PENGUIN BOOKS

ECLIPSED EMPIRE

Tessa Hale, author of love stories with magic, usually with more than one love interest. Constant daydreamer.

Also by Tessa Hale

The Wolves of Crescent Creek series

Crescent Kingdom

Eclipsed Empire

Rising Reign

ECLIPSED EMPIRE

TESSA HALE

PENGUIN BOOKS

PENGUIN BOOKS

UK | USA | Canada | Ireland | Australia
India | New Zealand | South Africa

Penguin Books is part of the Penguin Random House group of companies whose addresses can be found at global.penguinrandomhouse.com

Penguin Random House UK,
One Embassy Gardens, 8 Viaduct Gardens, London SW11 7BW
penguin.co.uk

Penguin Random House UK

First published in the US by Bloom Books 2026
Published in Penguin Books 2026
001

Printed and bound in Great Britain by Clays Ltd, Elcograf S.p.A.

The authorised representative in the EEA is Penguin Random House Ireland, Morrison Chambers, 32 Nassau Street, Dublin D02 YH68

A CIP catalogue record for this book is available from the British Library

ISBN: 978-1-807-83052-6

Penguin Random House is committed to a sustainable future for our business, our readers and our planet. This book is made from Forest Stewardship Council® certified paper.

FSC
www.fsc.org
MIX
Paper
FSC® C018179

CHAPTER ONE

Wren

WATER SLAMMED AGAINST MY RAVAGED BODY. THE liquid was so cold it felt like being stabbed by an infinite number of knives. But I still tried to catch some with my mouth. Just a tiny mouthful, anything to quench the burning thirst cracking my lips and throat.

Everything hurt.

It was the kind of pain that rivaled the worst my father had inflicted on me. The type that penetrated even my shifter abilities. Because, at some point, it'd become too much for my wolf.

I'd called on her when I first woke, trying to shift so I could tear the assholes limb from limb. But they hadn't just stabbed me. They'd also drugged me. And whatever they kept injecting me with made it so I couldn't call on my wolf half.

More than that, it made me fuzzy and unable to pull together a plan to escape. The fuzziness was fading slightly, though, which was good. I would have a few precious minutes to gather intel.

But the clarity also meant that I felt every ounce of pain.

My clothes hung off me in tattered slashes of fabric. My white tank top is coated in a mix of red, rust, and pink blood, in various stages of drying. At least my jeans hid the worst of it.

My legs trembled and nearly gave way, but I sent all my strength to them, trying to stay upright. If I didn't, it would be so much worse.

A hook hung from the ceiling of the empty warehouse, its attached chain making squeaking noises with every tiny movement. The monsters had chained my wrists and hung me from it. If my legs gave way, my arms would pay the price. Again.

Just thinking about it made my shoulders ache. One had already dislocated, and the man they called Angus popped it back into place. It was the one time I hadn't been able to hold back my scream.

I scanned the room around me, squinting into the dark. The darkness reached out with clawing tentacles, trying to strangle me. I fought back the panic and fear, focusing instead on the tiny sliver of light sneaking under a door in the far wall.

It was my only comfort now.

Pain racked my body, but it wasn't from the many wounds. It was much worse.

It was the agony of rejection.

Kingston's face flashed in my mind. The hurt. The betrayal. The accusations.

Brix's haunted eyes swirled in my imagination then. The confused pain.

And Ender. The sheer pleasure at finding the evidence he'd so desperately wanted. His triumph.

A single tear slid down my cheek. It was all I could allow myself—a tiny flicker of weakness before I shored up my defenses.

Focus, Wren.

Taking a deep breath, I looked around the room again and

used the physical pain to keep myself in the here and now. I had no memory of the monsters bringing me here. Didn't know how long it had been. One day? Two? More?

There were no windows to give me a clue as to where we were or what time of day it was. Nothing about the building itself gave me any information either. I pulled some air in through my nose, trying to tap into my fading shifter senses.

I could smell my blood, the metallic tinge coating my throat. But I tried to search past that. Motor oil, grease. Pine. Lake water.

It could've been countless places. And the truth was, it didn't matter if I couldn't get free.

As if the universe were taunting me, the sound of motorcycles filled the air. My body began to tremble. There wasn't a damn thing I could do to stop it because my muscles knew what was coming.

The sounds cut off in waves, replaced by rough voices until the hinges on a door squeaked. I caught flashes of fading daylight. A gravel lot. And those bikes I'd heard.

Massive overhead lights flicked on, and I blinked against the vicious beams, the ache already thrumming in my head intensifying.

"Well, whaddya know? The Diablos' bitch is still breathing. I'm a little disappointed, boys."

I squinted, trying to get my eyes to adjust to the brightness. *Angus.* He wore one of those leather vests. The emblem on the back alone would've had me steering clear. *Death Walkers MC.* Below it was a skeletal face with its mouth open in a silent scream. On the front, Angus's patch read *Pres.*

He was undoubtedly their leader. Likely because he had the most meanness in him. His hair and scraggly beard were a mixture of red, brown, and gray. But his eyes? They were pure black.

I'd never seen anything like it in a human. But this man didn't smell like the supernatural world. No, he'd given his soul to the darkness, free and clear.

A dozen or so of his *brothers* spilled in, taking their places around him and joining the handful he'd left with me. They all knew enough to keep their distance and watch their tone.

Angus's boots clomped on the broken cement floor as he strode toward me. My body began shaking again. I hated the weakness. The fear. But I couldn't control it. I could only control my choice not to cower.

I lifted my chin and met the man's dark gaze.

He laughed. "She's got fire. I'll give her that." Angus pulled something from his pocket. Slowly, he unfolded a knife. I could still see hints of my blood on the blade.

I shouldn't have been surprised. Angus's fingers were stained black with grease and blood. His knife was just an extension of him.

Angus ran the tip from my chin, down my neck, and between my breasts. "Have you ever considered they don't deserve your loyalty?"

A few of the braver guys let out sounds of agreement.

"You would be beautiful if not for all the scars. They must be the ones who gave them to you. Why protect them? I'll kill them and make it hurt."

My mouth went dry as I pictured the guys. Their faces swirled in my mind, each grabbing hold for a handful of seconds before fading into the next. But my mind ended on Locke's. His face stayed. The tender looks that swept over him. The way his gray eyes softened behind his glasses. How he would do *anything* for me.

My wolf let out a keening noise within me. She wanted her mate. Her *mates*. Even the ones who'd rejected her. Though she'd likely rake her claws over their flesh once she recovered.

"What's the matter?" Angus singsonged.

"She probably had a stroke," another of the guys called, laughter in his voice. "She's been hanging there for four days."

Four days?

I'd lost at least two. The only thing that broke up the time was when they unhooked me and took me to a disgusting bathroom. But even that didn't seem to come in any expected pattern.

Angus traced the blade lower to my belly, occasionally pricking an open wound. "I'd almost respect her stubborn streak if I didn't need something."

Without warning, the blade was gone, only to be slammed into my side with brutal force. The air left my lungs in an audible *whoosh* as pain flooded my system. Lights danced in front of my eyes as I bowed forward, the chains around my wrists pulling taut.

My wolf snarled, wanting to be free. I tried to call on her and shift, but whatever drug they kept giving me was still too strong in my system.

"Tell me what they are," Angus growled.

He knew. Not the guys' true secret, but he knew something was up.

"It's fucking aliens," one of the bikers yelled.

"Shut up," Angus snarled, and the man snapped his mouth closed. The MC president held the knife pointed right at me. "Something isn't right about those Diablos. We know they're here, but we can never find their property."

"Cloaking," a deep voice said. "Gotta be some top-secret government shit."

Angus looked at the massive man as he considered that possibility, then turned back to me. He pressed the knife in right over my ribs. "Do they have some sort of tech hiding them?"

I didn't say a word, my eyes watering as the burn in my ribs intensified.

"Where. Are. They?" Angus snarled.

I'd never tell him. It didn't matter that half of them had abandoned me, rejected me, or thrown me away like nothing more than trash. I'd never betray them. I'd never be what Ender had accused me of.

Angus pushed the blade deeper into my body. "Tell. Me."

Lights danced in front of my eyes, and the room went blurry.

"I'll get it out of you, bitch. And I'm gonna make it hurt." Angus twisted the knife.

I screamed. And then the torture started all over again.

CHAPTER TWO

Locke

My fingers flew over the keyboard as I stared at the screen. My eyes burned like they'd taken a bath in acid overnight, left to soak like dentures in a glass. But I didn't stop. There were more avenues to take, more routes to check.

"Locke," Puck said, his voice low.

"Hmm?" I didn't look away from the screen. There was a bus station two towns over that Wren could've used if she'd hitched a ride.

The idea of her getting into a car with a stranger had my wolf snarling. It didn't matter that he was submissive; his mate was at risk, and that was enough to bring out alpha tendencies in anyone.

"You need to get some sleep."

My gaze flicked to my brother in the chair next to me. Puck looked rough. His scruff had gotten thicker in the last five days, and dark circles rimmed green eyes that had gone dull. Even his blond hair seemed to have lost a little of its signature shine.

I looked back to the computer screen, trying to find the right backdoor channel that would allow me to access the bus station's security cameras. "Like you've slept."

"I got a few hours last night," Puck defended.

What he meant was that he'd crashed for about two hours on my couch while I hacked into our local taxi company. There were no pickups around the time Wren disappeared.

Every single avenue I took came up empty. It was like Wren had simply vanished into thin air. But I knew that wasn't possible. She was somewhere. Or worse, someone had her.

"Locke." There was a bite to Puck's tone this time.

"I'm not sleeping," I clipped. "Not until Wren's sleeping with me."

My wolf howled this time. He was in agony, right along with me. We missed our mate. Missed her scent, her feel, her essence. Wren made everything in our world better. Without her, everything turned a sickly gray.

Puck let out a long sigh and scrubbed his hands over his face. "All right. What can I do?"

The tiniest bit of tension bled out of me at his words. I didn't have it in me to fight with Puck. He had been the only one who'd had Wren's back with me. "I want you to look for her in this camera footage. I just need one sec—there. Got it."

There were two camera angles covering the ticketing area. The bus station itself wasn't large, but they did a share of their business in cash, so it made sense that they had security. I was damn glad. I sent one of the two feeds to the monitor nearest Puck and put the other on mine.

"Let's see if she got on a bus," I muttered. If she did, I could match the timestamp from the footage to the transactions from the teller and discover where the hell Wren was going.

My gut twisted at the thought. I knew Wren leaving of her own free will was the best option, but the knowledge that she might've been okay with walking away from me killed something inside me.

The video began to play at four times normal speed. "Holler if you see anything that might be her. I'll pause it," I told Puck.

He nodded, his gaze remaining trained on the screen. "What are we going to do when we find her?"

Puck's voice had gone soft. Not with gentleness, but with defeat. Because we were going to lose something no matter what. There was no way around it.

"We go get her," I said, my back teeth grinding together.

His gaze flicked to me for a split second. "She doesn't want to be here. We can't force her."

Pain swept through me. "I know. We'll have to start over somewhere new."

"Just the three of us?" Puck asked.

If Wren wanted that, then yes. But Brix and King knew they'd fucked up. They would try to make things right. I just had to hope Wren gave them a chance to atone.

Ender, on the other hand, was still locked in his obsession with seeing Wren as the villain. It was like she'd gotten too close to his vulnerabilities, and it'd scared the hell out of him. So, he did the only thing he could. He went on the offensive.

"I guess we'll have to see. One thing at a time. We need to find her first." I reached for my energy drink. Tipping it back, I realized it was already gone. I kept my eyes on my screen but reached for my mini fridge and pulled out another.

"You're going to give yourself a heart attack," Puck muttered.

"You have your drug of choice, I have mine," I muttered.

Person after person flew across the screen. We had a fairly large window of time for when Wren could've been at the station, so it would take a while to get through all the footage. My fingers drummed on the desk, my body dying to move, run, find Wren. But there was nothing I could do.

Footsteps sounded in the hallway. I listened to the rhythm,

trying to decipher the cadence. They weren't quick and excited—the kind of footsteps that carried news. They were defeated. Both sets.

I didn't bother turning around as they reached the threshold of The Lair. I simply waited.

"Anything?" Kingston asked. I heard pain and rage in his voice, his words strangled as he desperately tried to hold on to control.

"Nothing," Puck mumbled. "You?"

"There's not a damn sign of her anywhere," Kingston said.

"She probably had a pack mate pick her up," Ender spat. "Who knows how many Red River bastards are crawling all over Crescent Creek?"

In a matter of seconds, I smashed my empty drink can and hurled it at Ender. He caught it at the last second, surprise lighting his features. I shoved to my feet and paused the footage. "If you don't stop with the bullshit bitterness, I'll hold you down while Brix removes your tongue."

Ender's amber eyes flashed gold. "You could try, but you'd fail. I'll—"

"Enough," King growled. "This isn't what we need. End, if you're still on this Wren-is-evil mission, you're on your own. You want to work with us, do me a favor and shut the fuck up."

Ender's mouth snapped closed, but fury still burned in his expression.

I would've loved for King to kick him to the curb, but the truth was, Ender was a hell of a tracker. And we needed all the help we could get.

"Where's Brix?" Puck asked.

Something passed over Ender's face. I swore it was pain. Or maybe regret.

But it was Kingston who spoke. "He won't come in. Not until we find her."

Hell. Of course, Brix would be taking this hard. He'd hurt

Wren. He was part of the reason she'd run. And if anyone was into self-flagellation, it was him.

Puck let out a low growl. "Someone must have seen her *somewhere*."

A ding sounded, and I turned, just catching sight of the icon before it disappeared. It was an incoming email, one sent to our general folder at Crescent Kingdom Security. But the subject line had my blood turning cold. *Missing something?*

A buzz lit beneath my skin as I hurried to open the inbox. My hand trembled as I missed the email the first time I tried to click. Cursing, I got it as the other guys moved in around me.

Opening it, I saw it had an attachment. A video. Nausea churned in my gut as I clicked *Download*. My security software would block any viruses, but it didn't block this attack. Not anywhere but on my device anyway.

The video opened to one of those boomerang images—a few seconds of a clip, repeated over and over. Wren. Hanging from a hook. Her body broken and battered. Soaked in blood. Strands of hair matted to her face.

And she wasn't moving.

CHAPTER THREE

Kingston

Wren. All I could see was her. All I could feel was the agony *I'd* caused.

My little warrior had been through so much already. A lifetime of trauma and torture. And I'd just inflicted more.

"Play it." My voice wasn't mine. The only familiar pieces were the alpha vibes bleeding from each note.

Puck muttered a curse as Locke clicked the play button with his mouse.

"Come on, Diablos bitch. No more fight left in you?" a raspy voice taunted. And it was one I knew.

"Angus," Puck snarled, leaning forward.

The president of the Death Walkers MC stepped forward into view of the camera as Wren swung from the hook, the toes of her shoes barely grazing a cement floor. Thick chains had been wrapped around her wrists and connected to the hook, and blood was everywhere. On her arms, her face, her body. There were even splatters of it on the floor.

"She's loyal," Angus said, amusement in his tone as he glanced at the camera. "I'll give you that. Funny that you broke up our li'l flesh ring when it looks like you've got one of your own. None of our girls looked as bad as yours." He traced a scar on Wren's arm with a knife, slicing into her flesh and making blood ooze.

A soft moan slipped from Wren's lips, but I couldn't see her mouth, her face. All that dark-brown hair—matted now—hung in a sheet and blocked her from view.

"She does make the best sounds," Angus taunted.

Puck shoved back from the desk, letting loose a stream of curses, his British accent growing thicker.

Angus grabbed a chunk of Wren's hair and yanked her head back. "Whaddya think, bitch? You want to play a little more? Show those bastards just how pretty you scream?"

"Go—to—hell." Wren's words were more rasp than fully formed syllables, but Angus heard her just fine.

He slammed his knife into her side, the force of it making Wren's body bow.

Snarls lit the air around me, and fur rippled over my arms. I wouldn't be able to hold my wolf back for much longer. Not now.

"Tell. Me. *Where.* They. Are," Angus demanded.

Wren's head lolled to the side as he released her, like she was too weak to even hold it up anymore. Agony tore through me. My mate. Hurt. Tortured. Close to death. Because of us.

Angus moved into her space. "You will break, but I hope not too quickly. This is too much fun." He grabbed her hair again. "Say hello to your fuck buddies." He lifted the blade to her neck, and then the video shut off.

No one moved.

I wasn't sure any of us even breathed. All I could hear was the blood roaring in my ears, pounding with panic and failure.

"She's trying to protect us," Locke whispered.

We all knew it. She was taking the pain so we stayed safe. *Fucking hell.* We didn't deserve her. None of us. But especially me.

"It could be an act. Faking it to get us to do something. They're probably going to ask for a ransom," Ender argued.

I whirled on him. "Are you fucking kidding me?"

I'd barely gotten the sentence out before Locke's fist crashed into Ender's jaw. He followed it up with a jab to the nose that had a satisfying crunch piercing the air.

"Fucking hell," Ender growled as Puck moved in to push Locke back. I knew it wasn't for Ender's benefit; it was for Locke's. As much improvement as Locke had made in hand-to-hand, Ender was a trained assassin and could kill Locke in two seconds flat if he wanted to.

"I'm not even allowed to state a possibility?" Ender snapped, grabbing for a paper towel to put under his nose.

"You can, but you'll have to deal with the consequences." My voice held no emotion as I moved into Ender's space. I'd gone completely cold. "And if you say something like that about *my* mate again, I will see it as a challenge to my alpha status and grant you the duel."

Surprise and the briefest flicker of fear flashed in Ender's eyes. My wolf loved the terror. It fed him, gave him energy for the battle to come.

"Is that understood?" I growled.

Ender's jaw worked back and forth. "Crystal fucking clear." Shoving the paper towel under his nose, he turned on his heel and stalked out of The Lair.

Puck's hand dropped from Locke's chest, and he ran it through his hair, tugging hard on the strands. "He didn't ask for anything."

At least one of us had it somewhat together and was thinking logically. Because he was right. There'd been no request. The Death Walkers didn't want money; they wanted vengeance. And they were using Wren to get it.

I stared hard at the screen, the final image up now, the knife pressed to Wren's throat. "We have to find her." Who knew how much time she had before Angus decided the best sort of vengeance was to kill her? "Locke, can you do something with the video? Find her location that way?"

He was already moving, sliding back into his chair, his fingers flying over the keyboard. "The video itself won't have a location, but the email might." Locke's hands blurred with how fast they moved. "If they sent it from a device, it may give us information I can track."

I hoped like hell these vindictive bastards were dumb and had left countless trails for us to find. Ones that would lead us straight to Wren.

"She's not healing," Puck said, his voice low.

"I know," I rasped. I could see that Wren's more recent wounds weren't closing like they should have. It could happen when our systems were overloaded. When there was just too much damage. It meant she didn't have the same kind of protections she'd typically have.

Puck squeezed the back of his neck hard. "And she's not shifting."

I knew that, too. It meant she was too weak. Too drained. Too close to death.

"I can't lose her," Puck whispered.

My eyes burned with the worst kind of pain. "That's not going to happen."

I spoke the words with a certainty I didn't feel, hoping I could somehow speak the outcome into existence.

The typing stopped, sending Puck's and my focus back to Locke and his computer. "What?" I demanded.

Locke simply stared at the screen for a long moment, then slowly turned around. "The IP address from that email?"

"Yeah? Where's it coming from?" Puck demanded.

Locke looked up at him. "Inside Arcane."

CHAPTER FOUR

Puck

I WAS MOVING BEFORE I CONSIDERED THE WISDOM OF IT, taking off down the hallway as shouts sounded behind me. Those assholes had been in Arcane. *My* bar.

My boots hit the carpeted hardwood in a vicious tempo. Gods, I hoped like hell they were still there. I'd slit their throats and not give a damn if the whole town saw.

As I reached for the doorknob, a hand grabbed my tee and pulled me back. "Take a breath," Kingston clipped.

"A breath?" I snarled. "Wren is hanging from a goddamned hook. They're draining all the blood from her body, and you want me to…what? Meditate?"

King shoved me, trying to jerk me to attention. "No. I want you to not get dead." His light-blue eyes went pure silver. "Did you ever think that they might be laying a trap? Hoping we'll all come running so they can take us out one by one?"

Unease slid through me as I thought about my staff at Arcane.

Dina and Gary were on today, trying to hold it together after Wren and I bailed on them. They just didn't know why.

"Fuck," I muttered.

"Exactly."

I pressed the heels of my palms to my eyes, trying to relieve some of the pressure in my head. "What do we do?"

"We go there, but we make the approach smart. We don't go in the way we usually do. We circle until we know for sure there aren't traps."

I dropped my hands from my face. "Okay. One vehicle or two?"

"I'll take the SUV. You grab your bike. It'll give us flexibility."

This was one of the reasons King was alpha. His brain was always strategizing. And having my bike could become necessary going up against an MC. If they were on bikes, too, they could dodge, weave, and get through tight spaces. One of us needed to be able to, as well.

"Let's move," I clipped.

King pulled out his phone, his fingers flying across the screen. "Locke sent us a still from the video with Wren blurred out. Once we clear Arcane, we need to ask around and see if anyone recognizes the building and knows where it is. If they sent the email from the bar, she's close."

My gut twisted in a vicious jerk. Wren. My mate. Hurting. *Dying.* So close but somehow beyond our reach.

I shoved the thoughts from my mind and strode out the front door, moving toward the massive garage on the side of the house. King had already hit *Open* from the app on his phone for the bay doors in front of his dark SUV and the row of motorcycles.

If I'd been going for a pleasure ride, I would've gone for the Triumph. But this was far from fun. I needed speed and precision, so I went straight for the Ducati Panigale. The red paint job with its custom accents wasn't exactly subtle, but there wasn't a damn thing I could do about it now.

Moving to the side of the garage, I grabbed my leather jacket and helmet. Donning both, I climbed on and started my girl up.

"*Ready?*" King's voice filled my mind.

"*Tell me the approach you want.*"

"*I'll head in clockwise, approaching Arcane from the south. You go counter and approach from the west.*"

Neither was our typical route, and that was the point. *"See you there."*

The SUV's engine started up, but I was already out of the garage. I didn't waste any time. My hand twisted the throttle, taking me off the property in a flash. The speed was a combination of desperate need and strategy.

You could easily determine if you were being followed if you went fast. But it also meant getting to leads quicker. And that mattered the most. Finding Wren.

My bike hugged every curve in the road. Knowing it would take King longer to make his loop, I swung through a more rundown part of town, looking for anything out of place. Bikes that were too nice, unfamiliar faces, scents that didn't belong.

But I didn't see a damn thing that said Wren could be there.

Letting out a growl of frustration, I turned my bike toward Arcane. I focused all my senses, readying myself for an attack, but nothing came.

I dropped my speed and eased into the bar's parking lot. Shutting off the Ducati's engine, I climbed off. As I took off my helmet, I realized things wouldn't remain attack-free.

Red hair caught the sunlight as Cressida moved in my direction. My wolf let out a low growl. He didn't want the female who'd been so cruel to Wren anywhere near us, and I agreed. Cress was dressed immaculately—not over-the-top, but she'd certainly put in some effort: jeans that hugged every curve with a shirt that made sure I knew exactly what was underneath.

"Puck," she greeted, her voice soft in a way that was all lies. She tried to play the submissive when she was anything but.

"I don't have time, Cress." I started toward the door.

She moved into my path, hurt brimming in her green eyes. "I wanted to apologize. Set things right. I shouldn't have tipped the waitress's tray. I admit it; I was jealous."

I gnashed my back teeth. Cressida wouldn't even say Wren's name. "It's not me you have to apologize to."

Cressida's lips pressed into a thin line. "We shared something special—"

"We shared a fuck. I was wasted. You weren't exactly sober either. It never should've happened. I'm sorry if that hurts you, but it's the truth. But maybe this is all my fault for not saying it from the beginning."

Just one more thing where I was to blame.

Shock then anger flashed in Cressida's eyes. "Has anyone told you what a bastard you are?"

"Not today," I muttered.

"Fuck off, Puck," Cressida clipped and then stalked away.

"Jesus." I squeezed the bridge of my nose.

"More problems?" King asked as he walked up.

"Not important." None of it was. Nothing but Wren.

"I didn't see anything on my approach. You?"

I shook my head. "Everything's quiet."

"I don't like it," King gritted out.

"Me either."

I stalked to the door and hauled it open. At four o'clock, it was that lull between lunch and dinner, and only a few patrons were inside. Dina looked up from behind the bar, her eyes flashing with frustration and worry, but she waited until we were close to speak.

"What the hell is going on?"

I winced. "I'm sorry, D. I—"

"You bail on me, and Wren's in the wind. Did you hurt her?"

King and I shared a look.

Dina let out a low growl that had my wolf nodding in respect. "Do I need to take my bat to you?"

Honestly, her bat would've been a welcome reprieve. I'd take the physical pain over the emotional any day of the week.

"There's some stuff going on that we can't talk about," I said, my voice low.

Dina's whole demeanor shifted. "She in trouble?"

I nodded. "Did you see anyone in here today who read *MC* to you?"

Dina's shoulders straightened. "Two guys came for a late lunch. Wore cuts. Read like supreme assholes."

King's jaw worked back and forth. "You get a look at their bikes?"

Dina shook her head. "No. Didn't go outside while they were here. Did they hurt Wren?"

"We don't know," Kingston said, his voice low. I admired the restraint and mask he held on to so expertly. "But we've got a lead. Do you know where this building is?"

Kingston flipped his phone around so Dina could see the screen. Locke had erased Wren from the photo, blurring the center of it and darkening the section so you'd never know a woman was there. Though not just any woman.

Wren.

Pain clawed at me, taking vicious swipes. I just let it come. I deserved it. We all did. For not protecting Wren. For making her run in the first place.

"No...I don't think I've ever seen it before. You got a photo of the outside?" Dina asked Kingston.

"I wish I did." Fatigue oozed from King's words as he shoved the phone into his pocket.

"Ask Clyde," Dina suggested. "He's lived here forever. Might know where it is."

Kingston lifted his chin in agreement. "Good idea." He turned to me. "You gonna be okay?"

I jerked my head in a nod. "Let me know what Clyde says."

Kingston was already moving, needing to do something, *anything*, to help bring Wren home.

"Did someone take her, Puck?" Dina dropped her voice so low it would've been hard to hear if I didn't have supernatural hearing.

I opened my mouth to lie to Dina's face but found I couldn't. Instead, I gave her the truth. "Yes. Someone took her. And I'm going to end them in a way that makes them wish they'd never taken their first breath."

CHAPTER FIVE

Kingston

My feet hit the pavement like jabs to a heavy bag. I poured my anger, frustration, and fear into every step as I crossed the parking lot and headed for Crescent Kingdom. We had to find something, anything, that would lead us to Wren. And the Death Walkers.

I'd always been one to encourage my pack to lead with mercy. Not this time. I would wipe every single Death Walker from this Earth. Wouldn't rest until there was no longer a threat to Wren in any form. And I'd pay whatever price necessary to do it.

Hauling open the door to the gym, the familiar sounds of sparring and heavy-bag work filled my ears. Normally, it was a comfort. But not today.

Today, nothing would soothe me except Wren.

The moment I stepped inside, Clyde's gaze cut to me from the side of the ring. Then, he was moving. The older man wasn't fast, given the injuries he'd sustained over his fighting years, but he was on a mission now. Everything in me churned.

We'd told people that Wren was feeling under the weather, but since she'd been *sick* recently, everyone who knew her was starting to get suspicious. Clyde's gaze swept over me before landing on my face. "How's our girl doing?"

Fucking hell. That one hurt. Wren had been my girl. For a fleeting handful of moments, anyway. But they had been the best of my life. Until I threw them all away.

"She's still not feeling great," I mumbled.

Clyde's eyes narrowed. "You know you're like a son to me, boy. But if you keep lying to my face, I'm gonna box your ears."

My hands fisted, and I let my claws lengthen just enough to prick my palms. I needed the pain to keep myself in check. Too much was at stake.

It wasn't as if lying was anything new to me. It became second nature when you had to keep the other half of yourself a secret. But this was different. Clyde loved Wren like she was his daughter. He was protective of her in all the ways she should've had growing up but didn't.

All because she'd been born to evil incarnate. Bastian Boudreaux. A monster. And the man who'd made my sister's life a living hell.

It didn't seem possible that Wren had come from him. She was too pure of spirit. But I'd lost sight of that. I'd let the shock of her origins sway me for a single minute—and that minute had cost me everything.

"Kingston," Clyde said, his voice dropping low. "Tell me what the hell is going on."

Everything hurt. The idea of concocting another far-fetched lie was more than I could take. Just one more mark on my soul.

I stared at Clyde for a long moment. The truth didn't betray our natures. The Death Walkers didn't have the first clue what we were. They just wanted vengeance.

"Someone took Wren," I rasped.

Clyde's brown eyes flashed with heat. "Why the hell haven't you told everyone? Called the damn cops—?"

"Because"—I cut him off—"the people who have her want to hurt me. Us."

I couldn't exactly explain that we hadn't called the sheriff because we thought dark mages had Wren. It would've meant sending law enforcement in to be slaughtered had that been the case. But even now, when we knew humans had her, my pack and I were far better equipped to take the Death Walkers out. If we could just figure out where the hell they were.

A muscle in Clyde's cheek began to flutter wildly, making the gray scruff dance. "It's someone you and your team took down."

I nodded. "An MC back east. They were caught up in all sorts of dark shit. Drugs. Trafficking. Murder for hire. We dismantled their organization, but they reassembled quicker than anticipated."

Clyde muttered a curse. "And now they have Wren?"

I nodded, the admission costing more than he'd ever know.

"Well, what the hell are you doing to get her back?"

"We have to find where they're holed up. We know they're close to Crescent Creek because they sent a threat from Arcane today."

Clyde's brows rose before his expression closed down. "What kind of threat?"

"It's not important. What we need to know now is where this building is." I pulled out my phone and showed Clyde the photo.

He squinted at the screen for a long moment before shaking his head. "I don't know it."

That snuffed out my tiny flicker of hope. There had to be another way to find the location. Some tech tracking Locke could do. Building records or some shit.

"How's Wren?" Franco asked, pulling off his MMA gloves as he walked over, Juan at his side.

"Tell my future wife I can bring her chicken soup," Juan said with a grin.

A low growl left my throat.

Juan just laughed. "Damn, you're a goner."

"You guys know this building?" Clyde demanded.

Franco and Juan eyed him warily before looking at my phone, not used to Clyde's serious tone.

"I don't think so," Franco said.

Juan leaned in, studying the image more carefully. "You know, this might be one of the buildings at the old metal scrapyard in Deer Lake. My boss had me go to their closing auction to see if there was anything worth salvaging for the shop."

Energy buzzed across my skin at the possibility. Juan worked for a local mechanic who also did restoration projects. They were always hunting for parts and pieces on the cheap. And I knew the metal scrapyard he was talking about. It had closed about a year ago and remained empty ever since.

It was a good forty-five minutes away, but that would give the Death Walkers privacy. They wouldn't be worried about us stumbling onto them accidentally. And the property itself was isolated.

"What's going on, King?" Franco asked, concern bleeding into his tone.

I couldn't tell him. Couldn't risk him and Juan wanting to come along to help. Not when we'd likely have to shift.

"It's nothing. Just a case. This helps."

I opened the pack link in my mind and sent out a message. "*I've got a possible location. Meet in the parking lot of Arcane. Now.*"

Clyde leveled me with a stare. "You need backup, boy?"

I shook my head. "No, we've got this."

We'd do whatever it took to get Wren back. And then we'd return every ounce of pain the Death Walkers had inflicted on her.

I just hoped like hell we weren't too late.

CHAPTER SIX

Wren

Everything hurt. My muscles. My bones. My damn organs. I was pretty sure Angus had punctured one of my lungs with one of his stabs. It was getting harder and harder to take full breaths. All I could manage were shallow, painful ones.

Even my skin was in agony. It felt as if they'd left me out in the blistering sun of the Sahara for days on end. Or maybe that was my thirst talking. *When was the last time I'd had water?*

I wouldn't last much longer. Even my wolf had gone quiet.

"God, she looks pathetic. And she smells," one of the men said. It was Angus's second-in-command, Dent. The one desperately trying to be as brutal as Angus.

Angus moved closer to where I hung from the hook. I could no longer stand. My whole body was slack now, my shoulders crying out in pain. But even that had dulled to background noise. My mind was protecting itself from the trauma and torture.

Angus ran the blade down the unscarred side of my cheek.

"That's the smell of death. Fuck, it's sweet." The blade pricked my chin. "What do you think, little devil? Are you ready to hurt again?"

Images of times with my father flashed in my mind. The pit. The dark. The whip snapping back and splitting my skin. Brass knuckles connecting with my cheek. The feeling of my ribs cracking. Being unable to breathe.

An open palm cracked across my face in a stinging slap. "Wake up, bitch," Angus snarled. "You need to feel every ounce of pain I'm giving you. You're getting it all because of The Diablos. Remember that. Those freaks you're so determined to protect? They're responsible for this."

A tear slid free, tracking down my blood-caked face. I wouldn't make it through another torture session, and I knew it. Maybe it was for the best. I would slip away into nothingness and hope my mom met me there.

Angus lifted his blade, the silver catching the light. But then everything went dark.

For a second, I thought I'd died, slipped into that nothingness. But there was still pain, which didn't make sense.

Then there were shouts. Grunts. Screams.

I tried to let my shifter vision take hold. To *see* into the dark, even though it terrified me. But my supernatural abilities had been drained along with the rest of me. Everything was fading.

But I was able to grab tiny snapshots—one by one, and only for the briefest moments.

An arrow piercing one man's chest.

A wolf leaping through the air and snapping another man's neck.

A bullet hitting someone right between the eyes.

"There's a fucking wolf," one of the Death Walkers yelled, but he didn't get anything else out before the scream. A green-eyed wolf charged and ripped out his throat.

Puck. Some part of me recognized those eyes. Pain and relief surged through me in equal measure.

Then, there was a flash of someone else in the dark. Kingston. Pale-blue eyes and dark hair. But he was almost unrecognizable as he held two guns, shooting with expert precision—unrecognizable because of the pure fury on his face.

The pops, cracks, and screams were deafening now. A bullet pierced Kingston's shoulder, but he didn't even flinch; simply whirled and took out the offending Death Walker with a shot between the eyes. There was so much coldness there. It was as if he'd lost all feeling.

Angus cursed and moved behind me, grabbing my hair hard. "They think they're going to rescue you, but just wait until they find your gutted body instead."

He lifted his knife, ready to plunge it into me, but nothing came. Nothing but a strangled scream as the hold on my hair loosened. Angus was the one dangling in the air now. Brix held him off the ground by his throat.

"I am going to bathe in your blood," he snarled, the knife tattooed by his eye flexing with his fury.

Angus's eyes bugged out as true fear bled into them. "What. Are. You?" he croaked.

"I'm the creature of your nightmares." Brix lifted his free hand in front of Angus's face and let his claws lengthen from his fingertips.

Angus started to whimper, his jeans darkening as he wet himself.

"Weak human," Brix growled. "Coward. Preying on the innocent. Never again."

"Please—"

Angus's plea cut off as Brix punched into his chest and yanked out his heart. He let Angus's body drop to the floor but kept hold of his heart, his hand dripping with blood. Then he let the organ fall, spitting on it as it hit the cement before bending to wipe his hand clean on Angus's shirt.

The sounds of fighting and shouts rained around us. Flashes of light permeated the darkness as some Death Walkers ran in hopes of escaping. But all I could see was Brix.

Fur rippled over his arms as he struggled to control his beast. His nearly black hair hung to just shy of his shoulders in a wild tangle. But his eyes… Those blue-green orbs had gone stormy in a way I'd never seen them before.

Everything in me warred. Pain and relief. Hope and grief.

"Wren." The word tore from Brix's throat.

Tears filled my eyes as he moved closer. My shoulders burned with the pain of dislocation, and my skin blazed with countless cuts. Everything hurt.

But none of it compared to the agony swirling in my heart.

"Going. To. Get. You. Down." Brix panted between each word. "Help. You."

He reached out.

"Don't." My voice was barely audible, nothing but a raspy whisper, but it still stopped Brix in his tracks.

He cocked his head to one side, his animal half bleeding through. "It's okay."

He lifted me from the hook, pain flooding my system so intensely that the world around me flickered in and out. "Hurts," I moaned.

"I know," Brix gritted out. "Gonna fix you."

But it wasn't the physical that hurt; it was Brix. The contact. The pain of his rejection just days ago. "No," I whispered as I faded. "It's you touching me. You hate me. It hurts."

And then I was gone.

CHAPTER SEVEN

Brix

I STARED DOWN AT THE WOMAN IN MY ARMS. I DIDN'T understand emotions the way others did. Didn't truly know pain, other than the release it gave me. How it was the one way I could withstand physical touch.

Except for Wren.

She had been the one person who could touch my skin without me wanting to die. And now I was hurting her. Her body was broken and bloodied, but my *touch* was too much for her.

Fiery claws ripped at my insides. The feeling was so foreign, something I hadn't *felt* since that day all those years ago. The day the Red River pack killed my entire family and almost killed me. The day I'd turned it all off—no more emotions, good or bad.

Until now.

Pain. I felt something beyond the physical now. Hurt. Not of the body but of the soul.

"We need to move. Now," Ender spat. His gaze flicked down

to Wren and stayed there for a beat longer than necessary before moving away.

Did he feel the hurt, too? Did he know his actions had caused this?

Only it wasn't just Ender's fault. It was mine, too. My hesitation. My mistrust. And all of it had nearly killed Wren.

"Brix," Ender growled.

"Let's go," Kingston clipped, holstering his guns. "Locke's getting the SUV, and I have a healer meeting us in our territory."

He didn't look at Wren at all, but some part of me knew it was because he couldn't.

At the word *healer,* I started moving. I might not be able to fix Wren's heart, but I could fix her body. My little warrior would live to fight again. She would regain her strength. And I would vanquish every threat to her well-being from this Earth.

Ender strode ahead, yanking open the door and holding it for us. Puck raced through it in wolf form, shifting the moment he reached the sunlight. His nakedness wasn't even a thought as the SUV screeched to a halt in front of us and the hatch opened.

Some part of me was aware of Puck pulling on some spare sweats from inside while Kingston opened the back door, and I slid in with Wren, trying not to jostle her. Even though she was unconscious, I couldn't bear the thought of causing her any more discomfort. It was too much for me to take.

Puck slid in behind me, still shirtless and covered in smears of blood. Pain ravaged his face as he cradled Wren's head in his lap. "Birdie," he croaked, a finger ghosting over her cheek.

Locke gripped the wheel tightly as the others climbed in. The moment the doors shut, he gunned the engine. The trip back to Crescent Creek and home was a silent one, all of us battling our respective demons. But I was only focused on one thing.

The feel of Wren's heartbeats.

I tracked each one with single-minded determination as if my focus would keep her alive. Keep her heart going.

Locke slowed at the gate and the other SUV waiting there. "Is that—?"

A window rolled down, revealing a woman with strawberry-blond hair and pale-green eyes sitting in the driver's seat.

"It's Hera," Kingston said, his voice tight. "The healer."

Locke hit the button for the gate and shot past it the second there was space. Hera followed. The woman wasn't familiar, but I wasn't exactly social. And Kingston had connections everywhere. He always knew the best of the best. And that was what we needed now.

Wren's heartbeats started to slow, and panic lit a fiery inferno inside me. "She's fading!" I yelled.

Locke screeched to a stop, and the doors flew open. I instantly moved, sliding out after Ender. Kingston was already at the front door of our house, flinging it open.

The healer quickly followed, her pale-green gaze locking on Wren. "Tell me."

Her voice wasn't quiet or loud, but there was an air of authority in it, one that demanded answers. Kingston gave them to her, and I was glad. I didn't think I could summon the words to describe what had happened to Wren. My mate. My little warrior.

"One of our enemies took her. Tortured her," Kingston ground out.

"What kind of supernatural?" Hera asked.

A muscle ticked in King's jaw. "None. Human."

Something flashed in Hera's eyes. "Take me to your medical room."

She'd never been here before but knew we'd have one. It was necessary for supernaturals since we couldn't go to human hospitals or doctors. We had to take care of our own.

I moved through the house, Puck racing ahead of me, but the world around me was fuzzy. The only thing I registered was Wren's slowing heartbeats. The way they pressed into my arms at intervals that became further and further apart.

Puck jerked the door open and flicked on the bright overhead lights. I didn't wait. I moved straight to the gurney in the center of the room and laid Wren on it as gently as possible. However, when it came time to move my arms to give Hera space to work, I found I couldn't.

"Give Hera room," Kingston ordered, his voice low.

I didn't move.

"Brix," Ender whispered.

"I can't," I croaked.

Hera moved to the opposite side of the gurney, her expression turning gentle. "Let me help her."

I stared down at Wren, taking in the dried blood caking her face. Her hair was matted, and her eyes were closed. A bruise had bloomed across her cheek. I wanted to rip out the hearts of every single one of those Death Walkers.

Someone moved closer, poised to act. My senses told me it was Puck. "We need to give her the best shot we can."

I tore my hands away from Wren's body. The action was like ripping out my own heart, bloody claws shredding it into tiny pieces.

But I didn't stop there. I couldn't. If I stayed in the room, I'd likely rip the healer limb from limb. Because she'd have to hurt Wren on the way to healing her.

So, I stalked down the hall until I reached the back doors. Tearing one open, I spilled out onto the back patio and went for the first piece of furniture I saw.

Picking up the massive chair, I hurled it against a tree. The wooden piece fractured into countless fragments. I went for the ottoman next. Then a loveseat. I didn't stop until every item of furniture had been smashed to bits.

"Brix." Puck's voice sounded understanding but worried.

"Go back inside," I growled.

"You know I can't do that."

Because they worried I'd slip into the darkness for good. Turn and never come back.

"You need to be with Wren," I argued.

"Birdie would want me to make sure you were okay."

I scoffed at that. "I don't think she'd give a damn if I went to the pits of hell."

Puck shoved me hard from behind, making me whirl around, then glared at me. "You know that's not true."

Agony swept through me. Feeling. It was a thousand times worse since it had been turned off for so long. "She didn't want me to touch her."

"Brix—"

"Not because she was hurt but because it was too painful to have my skin brushing hers." Because I'd rejected her. I might not have said the words, but my actions had spoken loud and clear. Doubt. Uncertainty. Retreat.

"Fuck," Puck muttered.

I'd never forgive myself for that. I couldn't. The only thing I could do now was serve Wren at a distance. I'd dedicate my whole life to keeping her safe. And that started tonight.

My canines lengthened as saliva pooled in my mouth. I could already taste blood on my tongue. "I'm going to hunt the Death Walkers. Every last one."

CHAPTER EIGHT

Ender

BLOOD. SO MUCH BLOOD.

Having the sort of job I did, the kind that included taking lives, meant I wasn't a stranger to it. But this was more somehow. Blood at every stage. Liquid and pooling. Dry and caked. Everything in between.

Hera moved around the gurney as she bit out orders for supplies. Locke and King moved at the speed of light to get them for her. But I stayed still, staring at the woman on the gurney.

I ground my back teeth as I tried to pull the pieces together, studying each injury. Wren's clothes were in tatters, letting me glimpse the abused flesh underneath. The scars and the wounds. Too many to count.

"I'll need several suture kits," Hera said as she washed her hands and donned gloves.

My eyes narrowed. "You aren't using supernatural healing?"

Hera's gaze flicked to me. "I have both healer gifts and a

medical degree. And if you look at your mate here, she's going to need both."

Mate.

The word was like a blade to the diaphragm. Inflicting the kind of hit that made it impossible to breathe. "She's not my mate," I gritted out.

Hera arched a brow. "Isn't she?"

"No," I spat.

"My senses must be off then," Hera said as if unbothered.

Those in the supernatural community with more sensitive gifts could sense these sorts of things. Healers, empaths, seers. They could feel when two beings had a metaphysical link.

But they could also be wrong.

I was holding on to that possibility with everything I had. Because I wasn't about to be linked to this woman. The spawn of evil. The heir to the Red River pack.

Hell fucking no.

"Hand me those scissors," Hera ordered, her gaze lifting to me.

I stalled for a moment.

"If she's not your mate, you'll have no problem assisting me."

I knew a challenge when I heard one. Mates were often too volatile when their other halves were injured or sick. They couldn't be trusted to help in situations like these.

I reached for the scissors on a medical tray and handed them to Hera.

"Thank you." She moved swiftly but carefully, lifting the hem of Wren's tank and beginning to cut. "Locke, mix those herbs. I don't want her to feel any of this treatment."

He didn't hesitate, just poured ingredients into a ceremonial bowl as Hera listed them off. But I couldn't take my eyes off Wren.

Hera gently slid the tank top off in pieces, forced to peel it back in places because the fabric had stuck to Wren's wounds. Fresh blood welled.

I'd never been averse to the substance, but I suddenly found myself queasy and scanning the room for the nearest trash can, just in case.

Locke handed Hera the bowl, and she began to chant. Sparks lit in the air, lifting and swirling before making their way into Wren's skin.

My wolf snarled, clawing at my insides, dying to get free. "What the hell are you doing?" I snapped, moving to stop her, but King grabbed my arm and jerked me back.

"She's helping."

"The bitch is hurting her," I shot back.

Hera wasn't insulted, she simply let her hand fall as the last of the sparks sank into Wren's skin. "They will fight her pain so I can do my work," Hera said calmly.

I watched as a faint glow lit beneath Wren's skin, the sparks flying through her system and battling some unseen force.

"Not his mate, my ass," Hera muttered.

I clamped my mouth shut and yanked my arm out of Kingston's grasp, not saying a word. But I felt the healer's judgment.

She tipped her head back, lifted her arms, and began another incantation. This time, a soft breeze picked up in the room, and it was Locke who eyed Kingston skeptically. "You're sure she knows what she's doing?"

"She's the best," King said, pain in his voice as he gazed down at Wren.

The breeze morphed into something else. Something cleansing. The blood disappeared into nothing, as if someone had placed Wren in a shower. The only problem was that we could see it all now. Every scar. Bruise. Gash. Scrape.

Locke sucked in an audible breath next to me, a pained

sound emanating from his chest. Kingston let loose a snarl that told me his wolf was battling for supremacy. But I was frozen.

Fiery pain blazed up my throat, and I struggled to shove it down. "Are these—do they look worse than they are?"

Hera's gaze snapped to me. "Are you stupid?"

My lip curled in a snarl. "This stuff can be faked."

The healer showed no fear as she met my glare. "This woman has been through hell on Earth more times than I can count."

She lifted a hand in the air. "From this past week." Injuries began to glow in a blue light. Ones on the surface of Wren's body and more below. Too many to count.

"Ones from long ago." More injuries glowed in a pattern that could've been beautiful if it weren't for the pain and destruction it signified. Hera lit up Wren's body by time of incident, different areas glowing and scars illuminating along with things we couldn't see.

That sick feeling intensified, bile churning.

"I don't know how she's still alive," Hera said, her voice turning gentle.

Locke bared his teeth at me. "Still think she's lying?"

The worst sort of pain swirled inside me—the kind laced with guilty barbs. No. I didn't.

"Good," Locke snapped. "Now, you can deal with the fact that *you* caused this."

My gaze swept over Wren's body, fresh blood pooling as Hera got to work. Broken. Bloodied. Because of what I'd done.

I moved then, needing to get out, away. I couldn't face that I'd been the reason for it all. I tore down the hallway, away from the sounds I heard coming from the backyard and toward the front of the house.

Stumbling out the door, I struggled to pull in breath. I trippingly made it to the tree line, where I emptied the contents of my stomach. But the heaving didn't stop. Couldn't.

I wasn't sure how long it lasted, but by the time I was done, my stomach ached, and my mouth tasted like death. But I deserved far worse.

Pulling my phone out of my pocket, I searched for a contact. This one had eyes and ears everywhere and a high price tag. But I'd happily pay it if it meant getting answers.

He answered with one word. "Speak."

"I need to know the truth about Wren from Red River."

CHAPTER NINE

Wren

FLOATING. THAT WAS THE FIRST THING I FELT. LIKE floating on a sea of puffy warmth. Some part of my brain recognized that wasn't exactly possible, but I wouldn't fight it. Because it felt *amazing*.

There was no pain, fear, or loneliness. Just peace and cozy heat.

Something about that thought had my brows furrowing, part of me trying to remember.

"Wren?"

That voice. It was a deep, raspy heat of a different sort. But it hurt. Because I wanted it, and it wasn't mine.

My eyelids fluttered. Each sweep let in snapshots of light, so bright it made me squint.

"Nice and easy. It's okay. You're safe."

Kingston.

His face slowly came into focus. The room, as well—one that had once been mine for a time. It was in the big, beautiful house

I'd wanted to belong in but didn't. Just like this was a man I wanted to belong with but didn't.

Kingston's pale-blue eyes looked tired, and the thick scruff covering his jaw said much the same. He leaned over me, concern sweeping across his expression. "Are you in pain? Do you need any meds?"

I tried to mentally assess. My muscles ached like I'd done an especially hard workout but I had no pain. I was tired, but other than that, I felt remarkably good. "I'm okay."

The words came out as more of a croak, but King's shoulders sagged in relief. He reached out as if to brush a strand of hair away from my face.

"Don't." The word cracked through the silent room, and I recoiled.

Kingston froze, agony replacing the relief painted across his features. "I'm sorry. I—"

The door swung open, and Locke's familiar figure filled the opening. "She's awake." He glared at King. "Why didn't you call me?"

"She just woke up," Kingston mumbled as he stood from the bed.

"I made you some juice. It has the herbs the healer recommended for getting your strength back." Locke replaced King on the bed, setting the glass on the bedside table. His hand slid through mine, and warmth filled me. "I'm so glad you're awake."

"Me, too," I whispered. Tears pressed against the backs of my eyes, dying to be released. I did everything I could to push them down, but a few sprang free.

"Wren," Locke whispered, his hands coming up to frame my face, his thumbs sweeping across my cheeks to wipe away the tears. "You're safe. We've got you."

That only made me cry harder. Because they didn't have me. No one did. Even though I'd made it through hell yet again, I was still unbearably alone.

"I'll leave you two," Kingston said, his voice low. "Call if you need anything."

And then he was gone. More evidence of that aloneness.

Locke leaned into me and nuzzled my neck. "I've got you."

That was easier to hear because Locke had never wavered. He'd always been right there with his quiet strength and reassurance. My hand lifted and sifted through his brown hair.

He pulled back to stare into my eyes. "I'm so sorry."

"It's not your fault," I croaked.

He moved then, reaching for the glass of purple liquid with a bendy straw. "Take a drink."

I pushed myself up onto the pillows, feeling depressingly weak. I accepted the glass and took a small sip. I wasn't sure what to expect from a healer's concoction, but it tasted great. Like berries and cream with a sweet aftertaste.

"This is amazing."

Locke grinned as if I'd told him he won the lottery. "I wanted to make sure it was delicious and nutritious."

My lips twitched. "Thank you."

"Of course. Puck's working on a light breakfast. You were in and out the past couple of hours, so we knew you'd wake soon."

That had me frowning. "How long have I been out?"

Locke winced. "Two weeks."

I jerked upright, nearly spilling my drink. "Two *weeks*?"

He nodded. "Hera—that's the healer—put you into a healing slumber. It only ends when your injuries are fully healed."

Healing slumbers were no joke. They took a lot out of a healer, which meant they couldn't perform them often. It also meant they were ridiculously expensive.

"How?" I whispered.

Locke gave me a sad smile. "King has many contacts. He pulled out all the stops."

My gaze drifted to the door Kingston had disappeared

through. Guilt and hurt swirled inside me in equal measure. King's tenderness only made the loss of him harder to bear.

"Is everyone else okay?" I asked, turning back to Locke. My memories of them rescuing me were fuzzy at best.

Something passed over Locke's features, and panic gripped me. "Who was hurt?" I demanded.

"No one," Locke said quickly. "Well, King was shot, but it healed quickly."

"Ender and Brix?"

The last person in the world I should be worried about was Ender, but I couldn't stop myself from asking.

"End's fine. He's out patrolling, making sure we don't have any other unwelcome visitors in the area."

I shivered at the thought. "Brix?"

Locke went quiet. "He didn't deal with you being taken well."

Tension swept through my muscles. "What does that mean?"

"He's hunting the Death Walkers. Said he wouldn't come home until every single one of them are dead."

CHAPTER TEN

Puck

I STARED DOWN AT THE TRAY AS IF IT WERE A CALCULUS problem. Studying each item, I tried to discern if I was missing anything. I'd spent the morning googling foods that were easy on the stomach since Hera had said keeping it light after Wren woke was important.

Scrambled eggs. White toast. Applesauce. Oatmeal with cinnamon sugar. Roasted sweet potatoes. Ginger tea.

I crossed to the sink where I'd put a tiny vase of wildflowers. *Who the hell was I? Wildflowers?* I didn't do this sort of thing. Not since Alice had fucked me in every way but the good kind. But Wren was…different.

There was no panic when I thought about letting her in. Only certainty that she was meant to be mine, and I, hers. Adjusting the flowers in the vase, I turned back to the island and nearly collided with Kingston as he stormed into the kitchen.

"What the—?" My words cut off as I saw the stormy look in his eyes. "What's wrong? Is it Wren? Is she okay?"

Panic of a different sort grabbed me, not letting go. It wasn't fear of letting a woman in; it was terror that something could happen to her now that I had.

"She's okay." King swallowed hard. "Locke's with her. He's getting her to drink something."

I needed to get the food in there then. But when I really looked at Kingston, I knew my brother needed me first.

"Talk to me," I said softly.

Pain like I'd never seen before swept across Kingston's face. "She'll never forgive me."

Fuck.

I set the vase on the tray and turned to King. "It's just going to take time."

"I've only messed up this badly once before."

I knew the time he meant. When he didn't get his sister back before she was plunged into hell itself.

"King."

He shook his head violently. "She'll never see me the same."

"Maybe not, but that doesn't mean she won't see you as something better. Something more real. None of us is perfect. I'm sure as hell not. But you can't wallow. You have to prove to her that you're here. That you're sorry. And that you know who she really is."

Because Wren was nothing like her father. Bastian Boudreaux was a cruel and heartless bastard. Wren had none of that in her.

King stared at me for a long moment, not even blinking. "Okay."

I clapped a hand on his shoulder. "Good. Now, get with End on those new perimeter checks. Make our girl safe."

Gods, that felt good. Right. *Our girl.* Just like she'd always been meant to be.

King jerked his head in a nod. "Take care of her."

"You know I will." Just like I knew what it cost Kingston to walk away right now. Even if it was the best thing for all of us.

As King headed for the garage, I grabbed the tray and moved toward Wren's room. She really deserved something more than the simple guest room we had her in now. There was space on the third floor we could easily turn into a suite for her. If Brix ever returned from his mission of death and destruction, I'd get him on that. It would be good for one of the psycho twins to have a healthier outlet.

Walking down the hall, I heard voices beginning to rise. I picked up my pace and opened the door to Wren trying to get out of bed as Locke attempted to convince her to get back in it.

"You need to rest," he pleaded.

"I need to take a shower," Wren argued, grimacing.

"What's going on?" I crossed to the bed, sliding the tray onto the mattress.

Wren's jaw clenched. "I want to get clean."

The tension in her words had my wolf on edge. "All right. We can do that. But why don't you eat a little first? It'll make you steadier."

"I already drank the smoothie juice thing. I'm good," Wren bit out.

Something was wrong, and by the look on Locke's face, he knew it, too. I moved into Wren's space, slid my hand along her jaw, and tipped her head back. "Talk to me, Birdie."

Her skin, a little paler than usual, was now bruise-free thanks to Hera. But the scar on her face was a reminder of everything she'd been through over the course of her life. Just like I knew a smattering of new marks had been added to the tally beneath the loose tee she wore.

"I need to get clean," she whispered. "I want them off me."

Fucking hell.

It took everything in me to keep my grip on Wren loose and not let my fury grab hold in a way that could scare or hurt her.

I dropped my forehead to Wren's and breathed her in, letting her scent of wildflowers and rain soothe my wolf. "These monsters don't mark you," I growled low. "You're perfect just as you are."

Wren shuddered against me. "Please, Puck."

The *please* did it. The pain of that request…

"I'm going to run you a bath, but eat something while I do, okay?" I pulled back, studying the fierce creature. My mate.

Wren let out a long breath. "Okay."

"Good. Because I worked hard on those potatoes."

Her mouth trembled as if she were trying to smile but was unable to get there. "Thank you."

I brushed my lips gently across hers. "I'll be right back."

I tore myself away from her, needing to get it together. I stalked toward the bathroom and heard Locke coaxing Wren back against the pillows. It was too much. An overload of everything Wren was feeling. If the mate bond had been cemented, it would've been worse. I would've felt so much more of her pain and fear. But I found I wanted that. Would've done anything to take some of it away.

For now, all I could do was run her a bath. Turning on the water, I waited as it warmed, then plugged the drain. As the tub began to fill, I poured in one of the healing tonics Hera had left us. I got the sense that she'd gone above and beyond the kind of aid she typically provided because she respected Wren's strength.

I didn't care why. I was just glad she had. As the tonic fizzed in the water, I moved for the rose oil and dried petals. Even though it was daytime, I lit candles along the windowsill. Anything to promote peace.

As soon as the tub filled, I switched off the water and headed back into the bedroom. My gaze instantly went to the tray. Wren had managed a few bites of everything, but not enough. "You need more," I ground out.

Wren's hand moved to her stomach. "It's too much. My stomach isn't used to it."

Locke glanced up at me, his gray eyes somber behind his

glasses. "I think she'll need lots of tiny meals for the next week or so. Just until her stomach gets used to food again."

Because Wren hadn't eaten in almost three weeks. We'd kept her alive via IV and the supplements Hera had given us. "Fine," I growled.

"Bath?" Wren asked hopefully.

I jerked my head in a nod, moving to the bed. Locke and I worked together to lift her. Wren was so weak. As she stood, her legs trembled.

I couldn't take it.

Bending down, I lifted her into my arms.

"Puck—"

"Let me take care of you," I gritted out. "I need it."

Wren's mouth closed, the argument dying on her lips as I carried her into the bathroom. She felt lighter. Almost as if a strong wind could blow her away.

When we reached the bathroom, I gently set her on her feet. Locke was instantly there. "Let us help," he said softly.

Wren nodded.

Locke's fingers went to the hem of her oversized tee. She lifted her arms, and Locke tugged the garment up and over. I hadn't seen Wren's body since Hera put her into the healing sleep. Some part of me had blocked the damage from my mind. Now, it was all I could see. Angry scars crisscrossed her torso and arms, and countless new ones were raised and red.

Each one was a reminder of the torture Wren had endured.

One thought and one thought alone filled my mind.

I was going to help Brix rid the world of every single Death Walker. And I would make their ends a living hell. They would feel every ounce of pain Wren had.

And I would relish every second of it.

CHAPTER ELEVEN

Wren

Puck's green eyes bled to gold as he glared at my torso. I had the sudden urge to cover myself and disappear. I shifted, turning slightly so I wasn't quite in full sight.

Everything about my body felt mangled. Ruined. My skin would never be the same. My body would never be whole. Just like my soul. Not when my bond would always be fractured.

"Don't," Puck growled. "Don't hide. Not from me."

I sucked in a sharp breath as he moved into my space and dropped to his knees. Puck's hands moved to my hips, gripping me gently around the band of my sweatpants. Then he leaned in, his lips ghosting over one especially bad scar.

Locke's hand curved around my shoulders, steadying me as my body started to falter. Puck's lips moved to the next scar. "I'd give anything to save you from these. Keep you from feeling this pain. I'd pay any price."

His mouth skimmed each healed wound as if he could erase

them with touch and word. "But you never have to hide them from me. From us."

I stared down at the man before me. So massive and strong yet kneeling at my feet. "They made you mad," I whispered.

"They make me want to find every man who's laid a finger on you and remove their organs one by one," Puck gritted out.

His fury blasted off him in fiery waves I could feel. It was like it was a living, breathing thing. "I don't want you to have that kind of hate. I don't want it to turn you."

It was the sort of thing that could ruin you. Twist you up and turn you into someone you didn't even recognize.

Puck's thumb skimmed along a scar. "You keep me from the edge. But I'll always want to protect you. Will always be willing to lay my life down for yours."

"Puck," I whispered.

"You have to know, Birdie. You changed everything." He leaned in and pressed his lips to my belly again. As he pulled back, his eyes had a little more green in them. His fingers hooked in the band of my sweats. "Let's get you into the bath."

That was a good idea. I wasn't sure I could stand on my own anymore. Puck gently pulled my pants and underwear down and stood quickly.

"Do you want me to lift you?" Locke asked softly.

I shook my head. "I can do it."

But Locke and Puck didn't let me do it alone. And, gods, that felt too good. Locke took one hand, Puck took the other, and together they helped me into the tub.

I moaned as I sank into the bubbles, the heat and something else seeping into my muscles. "What's in here?" I mumbled as my head tipped back onto a towel Puck had fashioned into a pillow.

"Hera left us with a healing tonic to put in your baths for a while," Locke informed me. "She said it would help you regain your strength."

"Good," I murmured, my eyes fluttering closed for a moment.

I needed all the strength I could get. Would need to train harder if a human had taken me by surprise.

Hands closed around my shoulders, kneading the flesh there. “You need to give yourself time,” Puck chastised.

My eyes opened again, and Locke filled my vision as he sat on the side of the tub. I didn’t turn to answer Puck, simply spoke the words. “I’m going to need that strength.”

Locke stiffened as Puck’s hands tightened around my shoulders, his ministrations stilling. Their bodies spoke the questions their mouths didn’t.

“I can’t stay here,” I whispered.

There were countless reasons why. Half their pack didn’t want me, and who knew which of Ender’s sources had figured out my link to the Red River pack? I didn’t know whether that information had gotten back to my father. I couldn’t stay here. Not anymore.

“If you leave, we’re going with you.” There was a defiance and certainty to Locke’s voice I’d never heard before.

“Locke—”

“We’re with you,” he growled.

Puck picked up his massage again. “He’s right, Birdie. You’re ours, and we’re yours. We go where you do.”

My eyes stung, the same burn lighting in my throat. The sense of belonging felt too good. But it was dangerous, too. Because it meant there was more to lose.

Locke’s hand slipped into the bath water, taking mine. “We don’t have to figure it out right now. You need time to recover. Take it. We have nothing we need to do at this very moment.”

I knew he was right. It would be stupid and reckless to leave Crescent Creek and the Arcane pack’s protection when I wasn’t at full strength, not to mention the threat of the pack’s alter ego they were known as in many circles, The Diablos. My wolf let out a snarl. She was furious with Brix, King, and Ender but didn’t want to leave them either. She also didn’t want us to end up in a madman’s clutches again.

"Okay. I get stronger, and then we figure it out."

Puck's lips pressed to my temple. "Will you let us take care of you? Find that strength again?"

A hint of confusion swirled inside me until Puck's hand slipped beneath the bubbles, his fingers tracing my nipple under the water. My lips parted as the bud tightened.

"Our connection will feed you," Puck rasped.

My back arched as I leaned into his touch. The lore said that every aspect of physical closeness helped mates grow stronger. Physically. Emotionally. Supernaturally. Every part of our being was better with that intimacy.

Puck's finger circled the hard peak. "Say the word, Birdie. Tell us we can take care of our girl."

My walls were no match for Puck. "Yes," I breathed.

A low, rumbling growl slipped from Puck's lips. "Locke. Help me."

Locke's gray eyes sparked with silver beneath those black-framed glasses, but there was also uncertainty. Something about that pricked at my heart.

"I need you," I whispered.

That was all it took for Locke—just knowing I'd asked for something he could give. His hand slid up my thigh in soothing strokes. My blood heated as my nerve endings came alive.

Puck's lips skimmed the column of my neck. "You smell like heaven and home. Everything about you is so damn perfect."

I tipped my head to the side, granting him better access, relishing the feel of his lips and the occasional prickle of his scruff.

"Tell me what she feels like." Puck's words were a gentle order, and Locke's eyes flashed again.

"So smooth," Locke whispered. His finger traced a scar on my thigh. "Her body is a map of her life, telling me everything she's been through to get to me. To us."

Tears pricked my eyes. "Locke."

Our gazes collided, chaining us there. "She's so damn strong.

Been through a war. And now we're going to make sure she never has to fight again."

I wished I could believe those words, but I knew life didn't usually play out that way. Still, I loved that Locke wanted to give me that peace.

"Higher," Puck ground out, his fingers twisting my nipple into a hardened point.

Locke's hand shifted closer, almost to the apex of my thighs, but he didn't take his eyes off my face, as if constantly checking that I was okay. That it felt good. His gentleness and care nearly broke me.

My hips shifted, needing to get closer to Locke's hand, to *him*.

His fingers gently grazed my slit, coaxing in gentle strokes. Locke hissed out a breath. "Silky heat. A dusting of hair."

"Fuck," Puck muttered. "Need more. Need to know how she feels inside. Every damn detail."

Locke didn't look away from me, wanting permission, needing it before he took the next step.

I nodded, my hips rocking again.

He didn't wait. His fingers coaxed me open, and I let my knees fall to the sides, resting on the tub. Locke slid two fingers inside me, and my head tipped back at the delicious feeling.

"Tell me," Puck ground out.

"Tight, strangling heat," Locke said, his voice tense.

"In and out," Puck ordered. "Nice and easy. Drag your fingertips down her walls."

Locke instantly obeyed. Somehow, their cadence worked together as if their bond made their timing perfectly in sync.

My body bowed as Locke's fingers curled inside me, and Puck twisted my nipple. My breaths came quicker, short pants of need.

"Faster," Puck clipped. Locke picked up speed. It was almost too much: the feel of them both after feeling nothing but alone. Puck's lips trailed to my ear. "Tell me I can mark you."

My whole body shuddered. I knew what that mark would

bring me. More pleasure. More connection. But it would also tighten our bond.

"Yes," I whispered. Because Puck made me want to be reckless. Wild. His.

Locke's fingers thrust in and out of me as I felt Puck's canines lengthen against the delicate skin of my neck. My inner walls fluttered in response to them both.

"She's close. I feel it," Locke croaked.

"Now." Puck bit into the skin where my shoulder met my neck.

The moment his teeth slid into me, everything was more. Sparks danced along every nerve ending. Waves of sensation crashed over me in an endless cascade. I broke. My body pulled both men into me as if it wanted to keep them forever. And my wolf agreed, letting out a howl of pleasure.

Locke muttered a curse as he stroked me through my orgasm, coaxing out aftershocks one after the other. Puck's teeth pulled from my body, and he licked his mark clean. I shuddered again. The brand would be the most sensitive part of me until it faded weeks from now.

I found myself yearning for that permanent mark, the one that would link Puck and me together forever. Only I wanted one from Locke, too. And, if I was honest, I wanted it from all of them. Even the ones who had hurt me.

Puck pressed a kiss to my temple. "How do you feel?"

My mouth curved. "Like my bones turned to soup."

Locke chuckled. "You're beautiful when you come apart."

My gaze locked on his. "Thank you."

"Nothing makes me happier than giving you what you need."

I just hoped I could do the same for them. That we could find some miracle that would allow us to make this bond work. But some dark voice in my mind told me it would never happen.

CHAPTER TWELVE

Wren

I WOKE TO THE SOUND OF PURRING AND PRESSURE ON MY chest, but the good kind. Not the type that spoke of fear and anxiety but of comfort.

My eyes fluttered open to see Princess's tiny kitty body curled up right over my heart. Everything in me melted. Locke had told me that she'd slept with me every night I'd been in the healing sleep. And she stuck close even now.

Glancing at the clock, I winced. Half past ten. Even days later, I was still sleeping far more than normal. But my strength was returning.

A folded piece of paper caught my attention. I grabbed it and petted Princess with my other hand.

Puck has breakfast for you when you're up. Don't think about skipping it. I'll be in The Lair. Love you. – Locke

My throat tightened as I read those final words. *Love you.* He hadn't spoken them out loud, but he showed me every single day.

I shouldn't have been surprised that he would give voice to them in the most Locke-like way possible.

But still, fear took hold. That love was a precious gift. And it meant there was that much more to lose.

Princess butted her head against my chin.

"I love you, too."

It was so much easier to give an animal those words. Maybe if my wolf had supremacy, it would be easier for her, too.

Princess's purring intensified as I scratched her little furry booty. I couldn't help but grin. "What do you think? Want to get breakfast?"

She popped up like a little meerkat, her head cocking to one side.

I laughed. "You love eggs."

Princess let out a series of meows and leapt off me.

"Okay, okay, I'm getting up." I swung my feet over the side of the bed, moving to sit. I waited to see if any dizziness came, but it didn't. Progress.

The only problem was that progress came with decisions needing to be made. When to leave. Where to go. Whether or not to let Locke and Puck come with me.

I shoved all of it to the side and pushed to my feet. I made quick work of getting ready for the day, Princess chattering to me the whole time. Donning leggings, a workout top, and sneakers, I was ready to go.

I walked each day. Locke, Puck, or both came with me. Sometimes, Princess came, too.

As if summoning her, she leapt onto the bed and then my shoulder. I laughed and stroked her chest. "My little parrot."

She nestled against my neck in answer, and we headed to the kitchen. Music played softly, some indie rock band I couldn't identify. My breath caught when I stepped inside.

Puck stood at the stove wearing dark jeans that hugged his

hips and a white tee that traced every plane of muscle. My whole body came alive, my fingers itching to trace his brand.

"Morning," he called without turning around. He slid two pancakes off the griddle and onto a platter, then finally turned to face me.

He looked better, too. There was color back in his face, and those green eyes were full of mischief again. "Pancakes, eggs, bacon, and Locke's healing drink."

My stomach rumbled. "Thanks, buddy."

Those green eyes flashed. "Birdie, what did I say about calling me *buddy*?"

I grinned as I slid onto a stool at the island, Princess still perched on my shoulder. "That you love it?"

Puck let out a low growl. "I'll show you what kind of *buddy* I can be."

My body shivered with a pleasant tremble. "I look forward to it."

"You'll need to eat all of this, then." Puck stacked my plate full of food.

"I'm not Ender-sized," I grumbled.

Puck shot me a stern look. "I know you share with that little beast."

I lifted a hand to stroke under Princess's chin. "She'll get you if you talk mean to her."

The cat hissed in Puck's direction as if to emphasize the point.

Puck made a bastardized sign of the cross. "Get away from me, demon. Did you know she swiped at me when I tried to cuddle you last night?"

My lips twitched. "Were you trying to move her?"

He pouted. "Maybe."

"Then it was your own damn fault." I took a bite of the eggs and realized they were flavored with cheese and garlic. I moaned.

"You keep making sounds like that, and I'm taking you right back to bed," Puck all but purred.

"Not exactly a threat, buddy." I broke off a piece of bacon and fed it to Princess.

"You're killing me."

The feeling was mutual. Puck and Princess traded barbs as we ate, but I knew they really loved each other. When Princess had her fill, she leapt from my shoulder and headed off to do gods only knew what.

"She's probably going to take a shit in my shoe," Puck muttered.

I tried to choke back a giggle because it wouldn't be the first time.

Raised voices sounded, and I frowned, trying to figure out which direction they were coming from. "Who is that?"

Puck was already sliding off his stool, and I moved to follow him toward the back doors. The voices got louder the closer we got. Locke emerged from The Lair, clearly having been disrupted, as well. We spilled out onto the back patio to find Ender and Kingston yelling back and forth as a massive bonfire raged in the background.

Only someone was moving around the fire—someone tossing various items into the blaze. Brix.

I hadn't seen his face since he'd taken me down from the hook. Now, my stomach cramped. He looked awful. His eyes were sunken, the hollows dark. His hair was up in a knotted tangle, and his scruff had tipped into unkempt beard territory.

But it was what he held in his hands that had a sick feeling sweeping through me. "Are those what I think they are?"

Ender's gaze snapped to me. "If you think they're heads, then yes."

CHAPTER THIRTEEN

Wren

I GAPED AT THE MAN I COULD SEE HAD A FERAL EDGE TO HIM now. He threw a head into the fire, but as it spun, I recognized it as one of the guys from the Death Walkers. He'd broken two of my fingers before slicing my thighs with a blade—and had threatened worse.

I couldn't find any regret that the man had been wiped from the Earth. I knew he hadn't only caused *me* pain. He'd hurt so many others. And Brix was doing them all a service.

He tossed head after head into the blaze as King and Ender argued off to the side. I could hear snippets of the conversation, each wanting to take a different approach to reining Brix in.

Locke leaned into me, his arm pressing against mine in a show of comfort. "When Brix gets like this, the only thing that helps is making sure the threat has been neutralized. He needs to make sure the person he cares about is safe."

My heart broke for him. The only outlet Brix seemed to have

was pain. It was how he made his way through the world. All he understood.

"It's his way of telling you he's sorry," Puck said softly.

"Nothing like heads in a bonfire," I muttered.

Puck's lips twitched. "Just be glad he didn't dump them on your bed or something."

Hell.

But as I watched Brix lay waste to at least a dozen, I felt a deep sadness settle over me. When he threw the last one in, I moved, crossing the space to get to him. But just before I reached him, two figures stepped into my path, towering over me.

"Don't," Ender clipped. "Not when he's in this state."

A muscle fluttered in Kingston's cheek. "He's right. Brix needs time to come down."

I scowled at them both. "What he needs is connection." And even though Brix had hurt me with his silence and doubts, I couldn't leave him alone. Because I knew what alone felt like.

"It's too dangerous," King ground out.

"I know what I can handle. Now, move." I barked the words, my anger at so many things bubbling to the surface.

Hurt flickered across Kingston's face, but I refused to let it in.

A low growl sounded behind them. Brix bared his teeth, and I knew that if these two didn't move, we'd all be in serious trouble. I didn't wait. I shoved through the small opening between their bodies as Ender cursed. But I didn't stop, I grabbed Brix by his T-shirt and tugged him after me.

He needed distance from the death and destruction. Distance from the pack tension. Space to let his wolf breathe.

I guided him to the stream as his anger, rage, and guilt raked against my emotional shields like its own kind of torture. Kicking off my shoes, I stepped into the water. "Bend down," I ordered.

Brix's head tilted to the side in that animalistic way of his as he studied me.

"Please," I said, softening my tone.

He did as I asked but kept a wary eye on me.

I pulled Brix down a little farther, dunking his hands into the stream. I rubbed his palms, clearing away all signs of blood, any reminder of what he'd done. The more distance he got from that violence, the better. I just hoped the guys were doing away with the bonfire business.

Brix's eyes closed, and he let out a pained noise.

I stilled but didn't let go. "Too much?"

He shook his head, his eyes opening again. That swirling blue-green held so much agony. "Feels too good. I don't deserve it."

"Brix," I croaked.

"Hurt you."

Pain—the good *and* the bad kind—swirled within me. "You did."

It wouldn't help to lie to him now. His wolf would know it, and so would mine. We needed straight talk. Honesty. Even if those truths hurt.

Fur rippled over Brix's arms, but I didn't let go. "Hate myself for hurting you."

I moved in closer, straightening but not letting go of Brix's hands. "I don't want that. I don't hate you."

"It'd be easier if you did."

"Do you hate me?" The question tumbled out of my mouth before I could stop it. I hadn't realized that it was the question I needed the answer to more than anything. Was there a chance they could all see past my lineage to who I truly was?

Brix's face transformed, softened. His free hand lifted, and his knuckles, cold from the icy water, skimmed down my scar. "I could never hate you. You made me feel again."

Tears gathered in my eyes. "But you don't want to feel."

"I didn't," he admitted. "It was too much. I had to turn it off or it would have drowned me."

I knew that feeling. The mounting overwhelmingness of

agony. I'd turned it off in the pit. In the torture sessions with my father and his men. It was the only option sometimes.

Brix gripped my fingers tighter and seemed to be at war with something. "My sister. She was the last kind touch I had before you. I held her hand as she struggled to live. I held her hand when she couldn't. I held her hand for hours after she went cold, the life slipping from her veins."

And my father, my pack, had done that.

CHAPTER FOURTEEN

Brix

I'd never said the words aloud. Ender understood because he'd been the one to find us strewn across the kitchen floor like the trash Red River thought we were. He was the only one who knew everything I'd lost. But Wren needed to know, too.

"They tortured us for sport. My parents. My sister. We watched as they killed our father first. Then our mother. But they played with my sister and me. Sick. Twisted. And I couldn't protect her."

Tears spilled out of Wren's turquoise eyes, tracking down her cheeks. Pain for me. For my family.

"All they wanted was money, territory. And they didn't give a damn who they had to end to get it. No honor. Never challenged our alpha. Instead, they snuck in during the dead of night when they knew half our enforcers were away on a training mission."

Wren gripped my fingers so tightly that I lost all blood flow. But it didn't matter. I had to get it out.

Ender came and got me out. Called for help. He saw all the destruction. The death. It's why he's so angry now."

"Because of what my father did," Wren whispered.

"Your father. Not you." I saw now what I hadn't been able to in the shock of the moment when we found out where Wren had come from.

She struggled to swallow, to get words out. "He's a monster."

And she'd had to live with him for half her life.

"He doesn't care about anyone but himself," she spat. "Only making himself feel bigger, better than everyone around him. Forcing the submission of everyone in his orbit. It's never out of respect. Only fear."

"Even you." It wasn't a question because I'd seen Wren's body. Saw all the ways she'd been broken. Maybe she was just like me.

A sadness swept into Wren's expression. And more than that—defeat. "He always seems to win. Gets exactly what he wants."

Fiery tendrils of anger surged along every vein and nerve ending. "He didn't. Not with you. Not with me. We're still alive. Breathing. Free of his clutches."

Those sad eyes lifted to mine. "Are we?"

There was such pain in those two words. Her vulnerable truth.

"I've been running every moment since I escaped." Wren roughly tugged a hand through her tangle of dark-brown hair. "Every time I thought I could be safe, he blew my refuge sky-high. He still haunts my nightmares. And I'm still afraid of the dark."

"Little Warrior—"

"I'm tired." Wren cut me off as her shoulders slumped. "I'm so damn tired."

I moved in, just the tiniest bit closer. "So maybe it's time to stop running."

"It's the only way I know how to stay alive."

Fucking hell.

Bastian Boudreaux had torn my world apart, but I didn't have to live looking over my shoulder, worried he'd come for me again. That bastard had likely forgotten I even existed. The moves my brothers and I made against him were covert. He had no way of tracing them back to us.

But Wren? She lived in fear every single day. It only made me admire her more. She'd fought through hell and made it out. She'd taught herself to fight, even though it wasn't part of her submissive nature. She'd been so damn smart to evade his capture.

"How did you get out?" The question tumbled out without my permission. I didn't have any right to the answer, but that didn't change the fact that I wanted to know.

Wren looked at the stream swirling around her feet. For a moment, I thought she wouldn't answer me. "There was a party. My father had just come back from a raid. Those were always the times he was the *happiest*." She spat the final word like a curse.

"He liked to take that happiness out on me." Wren's sea-blue eyes swirled in an array of tones, darkening and lightening as memories took hold. "He had me brought to him in front of the whole pack. Said I needed to be strong like him. That he'd make me that way."

A sick feeling rooted itself in my gut, but I could do nothing to stop it. Just like I could do nothing to change what had happened to Wren in the past.

"Bastian had me tied to a post and whipped me until the pain took me under. I woke up face down in the mud. Someone had cut me down at some point, but their party had continued, no one thinking about little ole me."

Images of the scars on Wren's back flashed in my mind as rage swept through me. Anger was familiar to me. It was the one thing I let myself feel on occasion. But the sorrow that accompanied it now? That felt completely foreign. And the power of it nearly dragged me into a shift.

"Everyone was drunk or passed out," Wren went on. "Hooking up or fast asleep. I knew it was then or never. The beatings were getting worse, and I had no doubt that he'd eventually kill me."

Fur rippled over my arms as I battled to hold my wolf back. He wanted to shift and hunt the one who'd harmed his mate. And I wanted that, too.

"I managed to shift, which helped with the healing. I'd memorized the enforcers' positions and was able to sneak past one whose girlfriend was meeting up with him while he was on duty. I ran and ran until I passed out. When I woke, I ran some more. I made it from Louisiana to Virginia before I shifted back to my human form."

Wren let out a long breath. "Stole some clothes from the trunk of someone's car. Cut my hair. Hid my scent like my mom taught me. Bastian didn't know I could do that. Those shields were the only things that saved me."

I couldn't hold back anymore. I moved into Wren's space and let the scent of wolf, rain, and wildflowers swirl around me. "I know I don't deserve your forgiveness, but I will spend the rest of my life making sure you're safe."

"Brix—"

"My only purpose. That and making sure you're happy."

It was Wren who moved then. Her hand slid along my jaw and into my hair, her thumb stroking the knife inked by my eye. And then her lips met mine.

Her tongue stroked in, and I couldn't help the growl that slipped free as I pulled her to me, my dick hardening to the point of pain at the mere taste of her. Everything that was Wren flooded my system. That slight tingling feeling swept through me again. The buzz. And the lightness that followed.

I tore my mouth from hers. It was the last thing I wanted to do, but I knew if I didn't stop, I'd be pinning her to a tree and taking her. That wouldn't rebuild trust.

Wren's chest heaved as she grabbed my shoulders to steady herself. "Brix."

"I'm yours," I rasped. "Whatever you need. I'm yours."

Something shifted in her gaze. I wasn't sure what Wren might do. She didn't run. She didn't grab my face for another kiss. She wrapped herself around me, her face burrowing into my neck as she breathed deeply. "I'm yours, too."

Those were the sweetest words I'd ever heard.

CHAPTER FIFTEEN

Wren

I WOKE TO WILDFLOWERS AND THE HINT OF PINE AND MINT in the air. *Kingston.* There was no note next to the tiny vase with its mixture of yellow and purple—tiny blossoms I knew were only found deep in the woods.

My fingers skated over the delicate petals as an ache took root deep in my chest. I may have begun to repair things with Brix, but this bond was still beyond fractured. Kingston felt like a ghost, barely visible but with echoes of him everywhere. And Ender was hardly present at all. He stopped in for the occasional meal but then immediately took off again.

I should've been thankful for the lack of accusations and thorny barbs, but I found the silence unsettling. Princess let out a meow as if she agreed. I reached over to scratch her ears. "I don't know what we're going to do either."

All I could do was take things one step at a time. Today, that meant getting back to work. I needed to earn all the money I could if I decided running was the best thing.

But I had a feeling if I bolted, I'd have three wolfy companions.

Shoving those thoughts aside, I rose to get ready. Thankfully, the worst of my injuries had faded to faint scars, but I certainly had new ones.

I reached up to trace a red line on my neck. The memory of Angus slicing into me battered against my emotional shields, but I refused to let it in. Instead, I traced lower, my fingers dipping beneath the neck of my Arcane T-shirt to the brand Puck had left on my shoulder.

A pleasant shiver raced through me at the contact. I grabbed hold of that sensation and didn't let go. I needed it. Had to carry it with me today—the reminder that not all scars were bad.

Opening my eyes, I took in my reflection. My complexion had regained its color, and the dark shadows beneath my eyes had eased. I'd tamed my hair into its normal glossy waves, and my eyes no longer looked quite as frightened.

I was ready.

I headed out of my bedroom, Princess bounding after me. Voices came from the kitchen, and the moment I stepped inside, all talk ceased as three sets of eyes moved to me.

"Birdie," Puck rumbled as he crossed the space. "You look good with my bar on you."

My lips twitched. "You love to brand in every way possible, don't you, buddy?"

Those green eyes sparked gold. "What did I tell you about calling me buddy?"

I grinned. "That you love it?"

Locke choked on a laugh. "It's his favorite word."

Puck sent Locke a glare. "Do not enable her, or I will hide all your energy drinks."

Locke pushed back his stool and rose to his full height. "You do that, and I'll hack your high score on *Candy Crush*."

Puck's jaw went slack. "You wouldn't."

"You don't want to come between me and my caffeine," Locke threatened.

A muscle in Brix's cheek twitched. "This could get bloody."

"And you'd love that, Mr. Bonfire of Heads," Puck tossed back.

Brix shrugged. "A little blood never hurt anyone."

I just shook my head and crossed to the island. "Egg and cheese sandwiches?" I asked hopefully.

"I know you love them," Puck said, moving to plate one for me.

I bit into it, moaning as the flaky biscuit, gooey cheese, crispy bacon, and egg all melted in my mouth. "I would marry this sammie," I mumbled, my mouth still full.

Heat lit at my back as Puck's big body dwarfed mine from behind. "Would you now?"

I nodded and took another bite.

Puck's lips skimmed the column of my neck. "It's good to know you're open to bribery."

"I need to get good at cooking," Locke muttered, pouring me a glass of orange juice.

I smiled at him. "You're good at other things."

A slight blush hit Locke's cheeks. "I got us new locks for your next tutorial."

My smile widened at that. So far, I'd mastered combination locks and simple key locks. But I wanted to get into the deadbolt and safe arenas. "Tonight?" I asked.

"You could do it now if you skipped work," Brix offered innocently.

I pulled myself out of Puck's distracting hold and scowled at the lot of them. "You're trying to bribe me into staying home, aren't you?"

None of them would meet my gaze.

"I'm going back to work," I ground out.

Puck sent me a pleading look. "You don't need to. We've

got plenty of money. I can hold down the bar today. You're still recovering."

I pinned him with a hard look. "I put you on your ass in the fight ring last night."

"She's not wrong there," Brix muttered.

Puck sent him a glare. "You're not helping."

"No one's going to help because I'm going to work. I'll walk if I have to."

That had Locke moving closer to me. "No walking needed. I'll drive you. We just…we want you to be careful and not overdo it."

I saw it then, the genuine worry. A little of my frustration eased. "I'll be fine. Sticking close to you guys. Taking it easy. I promise."

Brix had hunted down all the Death Walkers except the second-in-command, Dent, and two or three others. It wasn't as if they could fight us with those numbers. But I was still on edge about my father. There was no way to know if word had somehow made it back to him that I was alive and living in Crescent Creek.

Puck let out a grumbling sound. "Finish your breakfast, and then we'll go."

I hurriedly downed the rest of the sandwich and chugged my OJ before they changed their minds.

Loading into the SUV, Puck lifted me onto his lap in the back seat, nuzzling my neck.

"Shouldn't I be wearing a seat belt?" I asked, laughter in my voice.

"I'll be your seat belt," he grumbled. "I haven't had enough time with you lately."

I slid my hands into his hair, giving him the contact he needed. "Sorry, buddy."

He growled.

Locke let out a huff as he guided the SUV toward town. "You hogged Wren last night. I barely got to cuddle her."

"Puck is a fucking bed hog," Brix muttered.

"I am not. We just need a bigger bed," he groused.

They bickered back and forth all the way to town, but it was good-natured, and our bond deepening had warmth spreading through me. But with that came fear because I wanted it far too much.

I barely made it through the door before I was being engulfed in a hug. "Missed you," Dina whispered, hugging me tightly before releasing me and doing a head-to-toe sweep. Her gaze stilled on my neck, where one of the new scars lived.

She swallowed hard before forcing her gaze to my face. "Are you sure you're ready to be back?"

"I'm more than ready," I said, forcing a smile. "If I have to be stuck in a house with these three any longer, I will lose my mind."

"I don't blame ya, girlie. They're the worst." Clyde strode over to me, Juan and Franco on his heels. He pulled me into him and lifted me off the floor with the force of his hug.

"They're way too ugly to be in your company for that long," Juan said with a wink. "You need someone who matches your beauty."

Franco rolled his eyes. "What? Like you?"

"Damn straight," Juan said, puffing up his chest.

"Keep dreaming," Franco muttered, giving me a quick hug. "I'm glad you're feeling better."

"Thanks. I hope you haven't been slacking on your training since we haven't been able to spar."

"Never," Franco assured me.

"Hey," Juan complained. "Where's my hug?"

Puck shoved him backward. "Oh, hell no. I don't trust you within twenty feet of my girl."

Juan's eyes danced. "Your girl, huh?"

"Our girl," Brix growled.

Juan let out a little hoot. "I knew it!" He held out a fist for me to bump. "Get it, girl."

Franco just laughed. "Now, he's a thirteen-year-old at a slumber party."

Everyone descended into a round of shit-talking. It felt…normal. And it was just what I needed. But I couldn't help feeling on edge. As I scanned the bar, I caught unfamiliar eyes on me.

The moment my gaze collided with the man's, he ducked his head. My wolf instantly went on alert. I breathed deeply, trying to catch his scent and bracing for the aroma of wolf.

Everything eased when I identified him as human. As I studied him longer, I put together the pieces. A fly-fishing vest. Hat on with lures on the table. Travel book beside his plate.

A tourist.

Nothing more than a man curious about the scene I was making with my friends and mates. But it didn't ease me completely. I wasn't sure I'd find true peace until one thing happened.

Bastian Boudreaux was dead.

CHAPTER SIXTEEN

Kingston

My fists hit the heavy bag with nothing around them but hand wraps. It wasn't as if the contact would do any real damage. Not with my shifter strength and healing.

And I needed the bite of pain the lack of protection could bring. Anything that would keep my wolf in check. Who was I kidding? My human half needed it just as much.

Both sides of me were more than a little at risk of going feral. Because all either of us wanted was to eliminate any threats to Wren. We needed every dark mage and Death Walker dead—but Bastian Boudreaux most of all.

Just the name had me hitting the bag harder. The knowledge that Wren had lived through some of what my sister had was almost more than I could take. The pain, the torture, the breaking of her spirit.

The fact that I'd caused her pain on top of all she'd already lived through made me want to rip out my own entrails.

"Makin' any progress on those demons?" Clyde asked as he sauntered up to the bag.

He'd asked the same question every time he saw me since Wren woke up. Because I'd been in the gym every day since, taking everything out on the bags and in the ring. It was the only thing keeping me slightly sane.

"They aren't killing me today," I muttered, leveling the bag with a hook.

Clyde moved in to steady it, and I felt his gaze on me, assessing. "You ready to talk about it?"

He'd asked that every day, too. But I wasn't. Couldn't voice the shame swirling inside me. Instead, I just kept hitting that bag.

Clyde sighed. "You don't let it out, and it's going to eat you alive. You know that better than anyone."

He was right. I did. I warned every person who came into this gym with a chip on their shoulder that they needed to give someone the words, along with this outlet. If you had the training without it, you could end up in a world of hurt.

My fists hit the bag over and over before the words were torn from my throat. "I fucked up."

The sentence was barely a whisper, but Clyde plucked it out from beneath the music, the sounds of fighting, and the other gym noises.

"Everyone does. We're not perfect," he said, his voice low.

"Not this kind of fuckup." Guilt swept through me. "I questioned her. Doubted her. Thought the worst of her." I punctuated each sentence with a blow to the heavy bag. It took everything I had to hold back my full shifter strength.

Clyde studied me for a long time as I hit the bag. That was him, never rushing, never filling the silence simply because it was there. He waited until he knew just what he needed to say.

"You think it's makin' it better to lock yourself up in a stinky-ass gym, punishing yourself over and over?"

I stilled, straightening to take in the man who'd become like a father to me in all the ways that mattered. "First, my gym isn't stinky."

Clyde's lips twitched, but the hint of a grin on his face quickly fell away. "You think I don't see you trying to torture yourself here? Pretty sure you've gained ten pounds of muscle in the last week."

He wasn't wrong. I'd always been a big guy, but I'd focused on lean muscle. I'd bulked up considerably thanks to the endless workouts recently. "Torture's a little extreme."

Especially when I hadn't been through the things Wren had. She'd experienced real pain. I didn't deserve Clyde's pity.

His eyes narrowed on me. "You're hurting yourself. Working out to the point of exhaustion. Cutting yourself off from your friends and family. Disappearing into a world of self-punishment. I don't fuckin' like it."

I tugged at my hand wraps, unraveling them. "Noted."

"You messed up, fine. *Fix it.* But you're not going to do that by holing up in here."

"You sound like Puck," I muttered.

"Usually, I think that knucklehead is acting a fool, but he obviously has some sense once in a while."

I wanted to smile at that but couldn't quite get my mouth to do it. "I'm trying."

"Are you?" Clyde challenged.

My back teeth ground together. "I left her flowers this morning."

I'd felt so damn pathetic. Sneaking into Wren's room and leaving the wildflowers without even a note. And it wasn't like the blooms could magically heal all the hurt I'd caused.

"Flowers are a start, but you need to be around to truly mend something like this."

I bit the inside of my cheek until the metallic tang of blood filled my mouth. "I'm not sure she wants me around." And that hurt worst of all.

"Gotta find out. Slow and steady, but don't give up," Clyde encouraged.

I jerked my head in a nod, but doubt swirled. "I don't know if I'm good for her." Maybe I harbored too many demons. Had too many scars.

"The fuck you aren't," Clyde clipped. "You're one of the best men I've ever known, and Wren deserves that."

A burn lit along my sternum. "Clyde—"

"She still in danger?" he asked, not wanting my thanks.

The question hurt. Because I hadn't made Wren safe. Not completely. Not yet. "Yes," I admitted.

"Fuckin' fix that," Clyde barked.

"Working on it."

"Good. Now, go shower, pick up your girl from her shift, and make things right."

"Okay, I—"

My phone rang from where I'd put it on the floor by the wall. I stalked over to it, swiped it up, and saw Locke's name on the screen. "Yes?"

"Someone tried to get onto our territory."

Fear swept through me like an inferno lighting in a single breath. "Where's Wren?"

CHAPTER SEVENTEEN

Wren

RAGE CLOGGED THE AIR, CLAWING AT MY EMOTIONAL shields. It was almost more than I could take, even after reinforcing the barriers with everything I had. But that's what happened when you put five supremely pissed-off shifters in a tiny space.

I crossed the length of The Lair to the door I knew led outside. I knew it only because I'd seen it from the outside. Locke had covered the glass panes with some sort of blackout covering inside. The only light was the artificial kind.

But I needed the fading sun and some fresh air, anything to clear away the emotions battering me. I reached for the door handle, but a voice whipped out.

"What the hell do you think you're doing?" Ender barked.

I turned slowly, glaring at the grumpy man. My fingers curled around the handle. "Opening the door."

The glass-paned wood swung open as if to punctuate my point, and Ender scowled at me. "It's not safe," he ground out.

"You cleared the property yourselves. You know there are no intruders, and all this"—I gestured wildly around the room—"alpha male fury is giving me a headache."

I shouldn't have given him even that. It could hint at my empathic abilities. But plenty of wolves were sensitive to others' energies, especially submissives.

I breathed a little deeper the moment the fresh air hit me. I wanted to step fully into it and get some distance from the men and their anger, but I knew my mates wouldn't like that.

Ender growled.

"Give her a minute," Kingston ordered. "This would be a lot for anyone."

Shock pricked at my skin. If anyone defended me, I'd have expected Locke or maybe Puck. But Locke was currently ensnared in a battle with the countless cameras he'd put on the property, trying to locate an angle where he could see the intruder's face. And Puck was pacing back and forth behind him.

"Thanks," I muttered, dropping my gaze and letting the fresh breeze wash over me. I couldn't hold King's eyes. It hurt too much. Because I missed him and didn't know how to close the gap between us. Didn't know if I should even want to. Because the truth was, he could hurt me all over again.

Our circumstances hadn't changed. I still had Bastian Boudreaux's blood running through my veins, and Kingston had still lost his sister to my father's vile evil. I wasn't sure that was something we could ever get past.

"Then I should walk the perimeter," Ender ground out.

"I'd think you'd be thrilled if a sniper got a shot off at me," I spat.

Something flashed in Ender's amber eyes, but he covered it with indifference so quickly I didn't have a chance to identify it.

"Getting your blood out of Locke's carpet would really be a nightmare," he clipped.

That was more like the Ender I knew.

Princess let out a bossy meow, nipping at my heels as if trying to herd me back into the room. "Hey," I protested.

Ender's lips twitched.

I glared at him. "Did you tell her to do that? Do you have some sort of mind-meld with her?"

Ender lifted both hands in surrender. "Princess does what she wants."

I knew that much was true. I bent down and picked her up. "Enough with the biting. I'm fine."

She let out a meow that almost sounded like a bark.

"Okay, okay." I stepped deeper into The Lair but stayed in the line of the breeze, hoping it would help.

The rapid-fire typing stopped. "I got something," Locke said, his voice tight.

Everyone moved in behind him so we could see the screens.

There was a shot of the man from behind on the left monitor. Something about him tickled the back of my brain, but not enough to shake anything loose. On the right screen was a map where Locke had tracked the man's path. But a close-up of a face was on the center display. It was slightly pixelated, but I could make out enough. I sucked in a breath.

Every head in the room turned to me, even Princess's.

But I couldn't tear my gaze from the image. "I-I know him. I mean, I've seen him before. He was in the bar today."

A sea of growls lit the air.

"I want an ID. *Now,*" Kingston snarled.

Locke's fingers flew again. "I'm not sure the photo's good enough to run it through my software, but I'll try to clean it up."

"Whoever he is, he was smart enough to stay far away from the cameras, limiting what we could get." Ender's voice held no emotion at all. It was cold—just like the rest of him.

Puck's gaze stayed locked on me. "I remember him. Did he speak to you?"

I shook my head. "Dina had his table. He left not long after we got there. I caught him looking at me but convinced myself it was just because we were making a scene." I should've known better. I knew to always be careful when someone tripped my radar.

But I had to admit the truth. I didn't want to run. Despite the rejection still stinging, I didn't want to leave Crescent Creek. Didn't want to leave the men who'd come to mean so much to me. Didn't want to leave my friends and the place that had become home.

I hadn't felt like somewhere was home…ever. Because even when I still had my mom, we ran every few months, constantly starting over and inventing new identities. I was so tired of it. I wanted a place where I belonged and people truly *knew* me.

But that came with risks. Like the one before us now.

Brix's lip curled as he leaned closer to the monitor with the map. "Look at the path he took. He's making his way along the entire eastern perimeter. He's looking for weaknesses in our defenses."

Which meant one thing.

Someone was prepping for an attack.

CHAPTER EIGHTEEN

Locke

I was different from my brothers. Anger didn't find me as easily. Maybe it was my submissive nature. Perhaps it was that I wasn't a fan of fighting. But rage wasn't a state I lived in often.

Until now.

The fury coursing through me felt like hot waves of lava. Every time I thought I'd gotten it under control, a new wave would crest and smash over me. Someone had tried to infiltrate our home. And I had a sick feeling it was to get at Wren.

Just thinking the words had me reaching over and pulling her onto my lap. I pressed my face to her neck and breathed deeply. That scent of rain, wildflowers, and home swept over me, cooling the worst of the anger.

Her arms came around me. "We're okay."

"We need to find out who he is," Puck growled. "Who he's associated with."

I scooted my chair closer to the desk. Wren made a move to get off my lap, but I stilled her, looking up into her face. "Don't. I need you."

That hypnotic blue gaze traced the planes of my face before she nodded and curled herself around me. It was as if she'd been made for me. She fit perfectly into my life like a puzzle piece. And I with hers.

I pulled up the facial recognition software I'd designed. It was similar to how others worked, only it pulled from databases I shouldn't have had access to: DMV, law enforcement, universities, and even places like gyms. Anywhere that linked photos with names.

"How long will it take?" King asked, his voice tight.

Kingston had always been a master of control. It was necessary when you were alpha. But I could feel his hold on it fraying. He needed Wren. But he'd broken that bond.

"No way to know," I told him. "Could be ten seconds. Could be ten hours."

Wren held on to me tighter. I knew she wanted answers most of all.

"We need to make a defensive plan," Brix growled. "Whoever he's associated with could be planning an attack."

What none of us wanted to give voice to was the fact that the man could have also been planning to abduct Wren—the same way the Death Walkers had.

"I already have a call into the caster about strengthening the wards," Kingston began.

Wren straightened on my lap. "I can do that."

He instantly shook his head. "You're still recovering. You should save your strength."

Sparks of silver flashed in Wren's eyes. "Is it that? Or is it that you don't trust me?"

Kingston blanched, and the room went silent. "I would trust you with my life."

It was a simple statement, but we'd all heard his tone. The alpha bond bled into his words, turning them into a vow. Unbreakable.

The tension running through Wren's body eased a fraction. "Okay. I need to go out to where the wards have been placed so I can feel what's been put into them. Then I'll know how to strengthen them."

"Not happening," Ender clipped.

Wren glared daggers at him. "I like telling you you're not going to be an asshole, but that hasn't worked either."

Puck choked on a laugh and tried to cover it with a cough.

Ender sent him a dirty look. "It's not safe. Others could be out there."

"Then you guys can come with me. But I'm doing this." The defiance in Wren's tone said it was no use arguing with her.

Ender muttered something about *headstrong she-wolves* under his breath.

Brix moved closer to me and Wren, his hand reaching to caress her face. His thumb traced the length of her scar, up and down, over and over, as if he could erase it. The room went quiet again. None of us were used to Brix touching someone so easily.

"We worry about you," he said, his voice low. "Just want you safe."

Wren leaned into his touch. "I know," she whispered. "But I need to help, too."

Brix nodded slowly. "Okay. Together."

She let out a long breath. "No one's saying what we're all thinking." She paused for a moment, seeming to gather her strength. "This could be my father. It could be Bastian."

Energy crackled through the air like a living, breathing thing. Speaking Bastian's name out loud felt like summoning a demon from hell. Who was I kidding? I'd take the demon over the evil alpha.

"We don't know anything yet," King said, tension bleeding

back into his voice. "Could be someone the Death Walkers paid. Could be someone under the dark mages' control."

There was shadowy magic out there that could put humans under the supernaturals' control. It was the blackest of magic and came with a high price. But it *was* possible.

"Or it could be Bastian," Wren said, lifting her chin.

"It could be," King admitted.

"My sources are loyal," Ender ground out. "They wouldn't have leaked your location, even if they were in communication with Bastian."

Wren's gaze cut to him and held. "You have no way of knowing that."

His eyes narrowed on her. "I have years' worth of experience with them."

"You never know what can sway a person," she argued.

Ender opened his mouth to speak, but King held up a hand to stop him. "We don't know who it is, so we have to build a plan for every scenario."

Wren's fingers twisted in my tee. "He won't stop. Not until he has me. Not until he can make an example of me."

That foreign energy crackled through the air again.

"Make. An. Example. Of. You?" Puck gritted out.

Wren wouldn't meet any of our eyes. "He can't let someone escape him. Especially not his *submissive* daughter." She spat the word *submissive* like a curse or a bullet. "He'll want me back so he can torture me publicly. He'll want to either kill me or make me wish I was dead."

My arms tightened around her as if my hold could protect her from everything she'd already endured. I'd gotten pieces as Wren and I grew closer, but never the whole picture. I was getting it now.

"He's the one who gave you the scars," Kingston said, his voice going cold.

Wren lifted her gaze to him, so much strength in making eye

contact through her shame. "Yes. Him and his enforcers. It was a game for them: who could leave the worst scars without killing me."

A series of growls swept through the air, but I was the one who spoke. Because there was something I needed to know and understand to find a way to defeat the monster who called himself Wren's father.

"Why?" I croaked, that sick feeling swirling in my gut again.

Wren let out a shuddering breath. "Because I'm submissive. Bastian couldn't stand having a weak daughter. Said he'd beat the weakness out of me."

She pushed to her feet, breaking my hold. "But I'm not weak. Not anymore."

And with that, she stalked out of the room, leaving the rest of us with the brutal truth of her nightmares.

CHAPTER NINETEEN

Wren

SAYING THE WORDS OUT LOUD, TELLING THEM ALL WHAT I'd lived through—even in broad strokes—had let the memories get a foothold. They came in flashes like snapshots, but nothing I did could shove them back down. Not distracting myself with strengthening the wards. Not a pack run. Not the comforting embraces of Brix, Locke, and Puck.

So, I lay in bed, staring at the ceiling. Every time I closed my eyes, I saw my father's face. The way it would contort in rage as he called me an abomination. How he would spit on me, telling me the only thing I'd be good for was breeding. I shuddered, thinking about the cruel man he likely had in mind for me.

Sleep was not going to come.

Deep breathing and the occasional soft snore swirled around me. I could wake Brix, Locke, or Puck, and they would stay up with me. Watch a movie. Play a game. Whatever I wanted.

But when I looked at their faces, lax in sleep, I couldn't do it.

We'd all been stressed to the max lately, and they needed their rest. What I wanted was a run in my wolf form, but I wasn't a moron with a death wish, so I scratched that off the list.

I carefully pulled back the covers and slid to the end of the bed. Puck let out a sound that had me stilling, but he soon eased back into deep breathing. I stood and moved to the closet by the glow of the single light in the bathroom, then quickly changed into workout gear and headed toward the gym.

Even though the guys had Crescent Kingdom to work out in, it didn't surprise me that they also had a state-of-the-art gym at home. It was on the far end of the house with an endless array of windows so it didn't feel like you were exercising inside.

I silently padded along, listening for the sounds of…anything. As if my father might pop out from around any corner. I shoved that thought down. He didn't get to win. Didn't get to steal my life in an entirely different way than he already had.

A faint sound caught my ears as I got closer to the gym. A human wouldn't have been able to make it out, but my shifter hearing had no issues grabbing hold. It was the sound of gloves hitting a punching bag.

I thought about turning around and heading somewhere else—the library, maybe—but I knew books wouldn't help right now. I needed to bleed the anxiety from my body, and the only way to do that was through physical exertion. I prayed it was Kingston in there. He'd basically been ignoring me and keeping his distance since I'd woken up—other than leaving me the wildflowers.

As I stepped into the gym, I knew I was out of luck. Ender stood facing one wall, attacking the heavy bag like some pissed-off avenging angel. His caramel-accented deep-brown hair was pulled up into a bun, revealing the shaved sides of his head. But more than that was on display. Most of his body was.

Ender had ditched his shirt at some point and wore nothing but athletic shorts and sneakers as his fists connected with the bag. He was a sea of toned muscle, a faint sheen of sweat making the ink decorating his torso, neck, and arms glisten. The pictures permanently etched there were dark: a battle scene playing out over his body. Maybe it was a metaphor for what lived inside him.

A meow sounded as Princess trotted over to me, and Ender's amber eyes cut my way, his fists stilling.

My mouth went dry at the intensity of his gaze. "Sorry," I mumbled, turning to leave.

"Don't." The single word had a fury to it, as if Ender was beyond angry to even have to say it.

I stilled and turned around. "It's your house. I don't want to interrupt."

"Apparently, it's yours now, too." The anger was back in those flashing eyes.

"And that makes you mad," I surmised.

"Yes." He pulled off one boxing glove, then the other.

"You could always turn me over to the highest bidder." There were likely more than a few groups who'd pay big money for a chance to kill me or worse. And that was without knowing what I truly was. If my empath status became public knowledge, I'd be nothing but a slave for the rest of my life.

Ender's amber eyes bled to gold. "That's the kind of man you think I am?"

"I don't know you," I told him honestly. "But I think you're cold, calculating, and distrustful. I think you would do anything to protect the ones you love."

"Accurate." He tossed the gloves to the floor and moved to a row of martial arts weapons against the wall. "But I don't sell people out for money."

Interesting.

He grabbed two bo staffs. "Have you trained with these before?"

"I know the basics." My trainer in New York had just started me with a bo when I'd had to run again.

"Good." Ender tossed me one of the staffs, and I caught it easily. "We start out gentle. Until your muscles are warmed up."

I didn't miss the intent behind his choice of sparring weapons. These allowed us to fight without any true contact. A smile curved my lips as I kicked off my sneakers and moved onto the mat.

Ender did the same but with a scowl on his lips. "Why are you smiling?"

"You're scared of me." I wasn't sure what it said about me that I got such supreme pleasure from that. But I did.

The scowl on Ender's face only deepened. "The hell I am."

I twirled the bo in my hands. "You chose this weapon so you wouldn't have to touch me."

"Maybe you disgust me."

I arched a brow as I stretched from side to side. "Keep telling yourself that, Cat Daddy."

Princess let out a meow as she leapt on top of one of the treadmills for a better view.

A muscle along Ender's jaw began to flutter wildly, and I knew I'd gotten under his skin. "Stop stalling."

"Whatever you say." I pushed to the balls of my feet, readying my bo.

We moved in a circle, each releasing the occasional testing strike. Then we started to dance. The staffs made music as we battled, creating a rhythm all our own. Everything spilled into the movements: our frustration and anger, fear and uncertainty. And something I didn't want to look too closely at...*need*.

Our sticks crashed into each other as I moved in, trying to sweep Ender off his feet. But he was too damn good.

A chuckle left his throat as he snapped forward with a hit of his own, much more graceful than mine had been. "You've got fire, I'll give you that. But you need technique. Practice."

I struck out with one end of my bo, just missing Ender's shoulder. "I only had three weeks of training with these."

He arched a brow at that, a grudging respect entering his

expression. "You need time with the staff. Need to make it an extension of your body."

I could see what he meant. When Ender moved, his bo moved with him. They were one. It was the same with his bow and arrow. It was as if he could whisper to these inanimate objects and make them do his bidding.

Ender's staff struck mine, and he followed with a leg sweep like I'd attempted; only his was successful. My back hit the mat with force, pushing all the air from my lungs. Then, Ender was on me.

He straddled my hips, placing his bo across my neck but not pressing down. "Yield."

It wasn't a question, but I scowled up at him, refusing to give him that pleasure.

One corner of Ender's mouth kicked up as he leaned over me, so close I could taste his minty breath on my tongue. He pressed the staff lightly to my throat. "Yield."

"Or what?" I challenged.

Those amber eyes heated, but it wasn't anger I saw there. It was heat. Need. Want. The same that coursed through me.

"Wren," he rasped.

I felt the vibration of my name across my lips. And, gods, I wanted to lean into it. Wanted to close the distance and know what it would feel like to drown in Ender. To bleed out all our hate on the mat.

"You don't know what you're playing at," he growled.

I felt my wolf take hold, accepting his challenge. "Don't I?"

Ender leaned closer, just a breath away, and then—

Puck's snarl lit the air. "What the fuck are you doing, Ender?"

CHAPTER TWENTY

Wren

ENDER WAS OFF ME IN A FLASH, ANNOYANCE FILLING HIS gaze. "She wouldn't yield."

"Of course, she wouldn't," Puck clipped, Brix and Locke spilling into the gym behind him. "It's Wren."

"They call her 'Little Warrior' for a reason," Locke muttered.

Puck prowled toward Ender, anger swirling in his green eyes. "And the last thing she needs is you cornering her and not letting her up."

"Then you don't know the first thing about her," Ender spat, tossing his bo staff to the floor and stalking out of the room.

Puck moved to offer me a hand, but I didn't take it. Instead, I leapt to my feet, annoyance filling my gaze. "I don't need you to fight my battles for me. And Ender was right. He was giving me what I needed."

"An outlet." Brix's words weren't soft, nor were they loud. They were simply the truth.

Some of the irritation bled out of me at his understanding. I nodded and let out a deep breath.

Puck stared at me for a long moment before something shifted in his expression. He inhaled, his nostrils flaring. A grin stretched across his face. "It turns you on. Fighting."

Heat hit my cheeks. "No."

"Birdie," he growled, but there was a playful note to it. "I can smell you."

Shit.

The heat in my cheeks ignited to a burn. "His body was pressed against mine. I can't help it. He's my mate."

Brix's lips twitched as if he wanted to smile, but he couldn't quite finish the movement. "Have we been ignoring your needs?"

I let out a little huff of air. "Maybe. You all think I'm breakable after what happened." And say what you would about Ender, but he hadn't treated me like that. He'd believed in my strength, even if he was an asshole about it.

Brix's blue-green eyes sparked silver. "You're the strongest person I know."

Heat and pressure flared at my back, bringing the scent of Locke, all spiced hot chocolate and warm comfort. He leaned into me, an arm wrapping around my middle. "We're in awe of you," he whispered, the words teasing my ear as his hand slipped under the hem of my tank.

"But we should've shown you." Puck stalked toward me—a man on a mission. He reached up and wrapped my ponytail around his fist, tugging my head back slightly. Then, his mouth took mine.

No more gentle kisses or easy comfort. This was need, pure and simple, and it had a sharp edge I'd missed. One I needed.

I gave as good as I got, my tongue dueling with Puck's as Locke's mouth skimmed down the column of my neck. His tongue flicked out, tasting my skin. He groaned.

Puck tore his mouth from mine. "We're going to apologize now. Aren't we, boys?"

The gleam in his eyes had my core tightening as a rush of wetness gathered between my thighs. Brix let out a growl. "Your. Scent."

"It's like a goddamned drug," Puck muttered.

"Better than," Locke argued.

"Undress her," Brix ordered.

A shiver racked me as some alpha bled into his tone. I knew Brix was the beta of the pack, but it was clear now that he could've easily been the alpha of his own pack; he'd simply chosen to follow King's lead.

Something about the typically quiet man taking charge had my blood heating, even as that shiver engulfed me. It was the juxtaposition of it all. And the power.

Locke's fingers hooked into my workout tank. He lifted it up and over my head, taking the built-in bra with it until nothing but bare flesh remained. My nipples tightened in response to the cool air, and need swirled around me.

"Her leggings," Brix gritted out in Puck's direction.

He didn't wait. He dropped to his knees, his fingers grabbing the band of my capris. Puck didn't rush the action. He pulled them down slowly, watching in fascination as more and more of my body was revealed.

Puck's knuckles grazed my thighs, sending a wave of sparks crashing over me. My core tightened, wanting more, needing to be filled, stretched. By them.

Brix hissed out a breath. "So fucking beautiful."

"Smells even better." Puck ran his nose up my slit, and I nearly stumbled, but Locke was there to catch me.

Brix ran a hand over his length through his gray sweats, and my mouth went dry. He bit down on his bottom lip, nearly drawing blood. "I want to watch. Watch while you make her come harder than she ever has before. While you give our mate what she needs."

Locke pressed himself to me. His dick hardened against my ass, and I couldn't hold in my whimper.

"Those sounds," Brix growled. "I need to hear them all."

My breaths came in short pants as Puck lifted one foot and then the other, tossing my leggings and underwear to the side. There was nothing to shield me now. My back arched as I felt the power of that—the power of these three men wanting me so badly.

"Palm her breasts and tease those pretty little nipples," Brix ordered.

Locke instantly obeyed, his large hands coming up to cup and knead. His thumbs circled, and I couldn't help but arch into his touch.

Brix's eyes went hooded as he dropped his gaze. "Trace those legs. Tell me what they feel like."

Puck's rough hands skimmed along my calves. "Like warm silk. Taut. Perfect."

"Higher," Brix clipped.

Puck didn't hesitate. As Locke twisted my flesh into peaks hard enough to cut glass, Puck's hands slid higher. His fingers skimmed my slit and then delved deeper. He let out a groan that echoed around the empty room. "Fucking soaked."

Brix's hand dipped into his sweats. He freed his cock, stroking up and down, a bead of precum dotting the tip before disappearing beneath Brix's ministrations.

I couldn't take my eyes off him, watching as he stroked himself, that length growing impossibly. I whimpered again.

"She likes watching you, brother," Puck said, a smile tugging at his lips as his fingers explored me everywhere except the two places I wanted him.

"You like knowing what you do to me, Little Warrior?" Brix challenged.

"Yes," I breathed.

"Reward her for her honesty, Puck. Slide two fingers inside."

There was no hesitation. Puck stroked in, those two fingers stretching me. My lips parted, and I sucked in a breath. The connection, the feeling of them...I needed more.

"Tell me what her nipples taste like, Locke. I want to know," Brix gritted out.

Locke curved around me as Puck thrust his fingers in and out in a lazy rhythm. Locke's lips closed around a hard peak, his tongue swirling. He moaned, sending vibrations through me. "Like raindrops and sugar."

"Fuck," Brix muttered, stroking himself harder, quicker. "Another finger, Puck. Tease that little clit. But don't let her come."

The stretch intensified as Puck did as instructed, and then his tongue was on me. He flicked it against that bundle of nerves, gently teasing the hood back, exposing the most sensitive part of me.

I shuddered, waves of pleasure threatening to crash into me.

"Not yet," Brix snarled. "I want all your pleasure. Every last ounce. Hold on."

Puck stroked himself with his free hand, and I could feel Locke doing the same behind me. It was almost more than I could take. The scent of arousal rose in the air: need, want, and connection.

"End it," Brix ordered. "Mark her. Make her pleasure yours."

Locke's teeth grazed my nipple as he sucked deeply. At the same time, Puck's lips closed around my clit. It lit the final match, and my body sparked to flame. I writhed against them as my first orgasm hit. But it wasn't enough, not for my mates.

Their mouths were gone and then back. Locke's teeth sank into my shoulder as Puck's pierced my hip. Locke twisted my nipple with one hand while Puck thrust his fingers in and out of me with a ferocity that nearly had me buckling.

They weren't bond marks, but they were marks of possession, and I found my canines lengthening, wanting to claim them right back. But I wanted to make it permanent. And that scared the hell out of me.

Brix cursed as he came, but I couldn't see the pleasure on his face because I was already gone, lost to the sea of sparks and falling. But the best part of it all was that they were there to catch me.

CHAPTER TWENTY-ONE

Wren

"I'M TOO OLD FOR DELIVERY DAYS," DINA MUTTERED AS SHE sliced open the box of booze with a box cutter.

My lips twitched. "The hell you are. I saw you put that guy on his ass the other night."

A grin spread across Dina's face as she unloaded bottles of whiskey. "He was an asshole. Tried to cop a feel on a girl who very much did not welcome his attention."

D had kicked the guy's stool out from under him and sent him crashing to the floor before eighty-sixing his ass. It was beautiful.

And, gods, I loved that the dustup at Arcane was the most drama we'd had in the past two weeks. But the lack of movement on any front made me twitchy. Locke had at least found the identity of the fake fisherman.

Jackson Gilbert.

Man out of Denver. Worked at a car dealership. No wife or kids. And no known link to any of the Arcanes' enemies or mine.

It was possible he'd simply been a hired gun of some sort, but there should've been a trail. We'd found nothing. No one was happy about that.

Still, we'd managed to settle into a routine of sorts. I never went anywhere alone, but I found I didn't mind it as much as I thought I would. Having Locke, Puck, or Brix with me was comforting. King continued to keep his distance but left little gifts behind for me to find.

It was most often wildflowers, ones I could scent he'd picked himself. There was a vase behind the bar with them right now. Occasionally, it was other things: a new knife that was currently tucked into the pocket of my jeans, a caster's spell book on wards, a cupcake from the local bakery—things that told me he was thinking about me.

The only thing he hadn't given me were his words. An honest conversation about what he felt or didn't.

Ender had avoided me like the plague unless he was tasked with my protection. He was on duty today and chose to spend that time patrolling the block Arcane was on instead of sitting at the bar like Locke, King, and Brix did, or behind it like Puck.

Dina let out a whistle. "Earth to Wren."

I shook my head. "Sorry. Apparently, breaking down boxes takes me to la-la land."

Dina chuckled. "I don't blame you. But there are only two more."

"There is a God in heaven."

"I think we deserve a reward after this. Maybe I'll send Gary to the bakery to get us cupcakes."

The memory of the lemon blueberry one King had gotten me played on my tongue. "You know he lives for the chocolate peanut butter ones, so you likely won't get any arguments from him."

"It's the triple chocolate for me all the way," Dina said.

I broke down the final box as she put the last liquor bottle where it needed to be. "Done."

"Let's get these out to the recycling, and then it's cupcake city."

I wouldn't argue with her. We loaded ourselves up with cardboard and made it down the hallway.

"I'll get it," Gary called, lumbering out of the kitchen where he was preparing for the lunch crowd.

"How do you feel about a mission, Gar?" Dina asked as she maneuvered outside.

"Depends," he answered warily. "Is it burying a body or a trip to the store?"

A laugh bubbled out of me. "Why do I feel like you'd do better with the body?"

His lips twitched, the gray scruff around them dancing with the movement. "Hate crowds. Don't mind blood."

"Good to know," Dina muttered. "What about a cupcake mission?"

Gary's eyes lit up. "I'm in."

"Grab some cash from the register and get a dozen," Dina instructed.

But Gary was already moving back inside, faster than I'd seen him hustle in a while. I shook my head. "Good to know what motivates him."

"Seriously."

I hoisted open the massive recycling bin. The jumbo size was necessary with all the bottles and cans we went through. As I hoisted the cardboard into it, my shifter hearing picked up on something. Soft footsteps on the pavement.

I whirled, my hand going for my pocket, ready to pull my new knife, but I eased when I saw Cressida making her way down the back alley. Annoyance filled her green eyes. "I thought maybe you'd left. Haven't seen you around much."

There was no missing the disappointment in those words.

"Been here. Working." I left out the fact that she hadn't seen me because she was no longer allowed inside Arcane after purposely spilling her drink on me.

Cressida's mouth flattened into a thin line. "Look. Will you just tell Puck to let me back in the bar? This is so stupid."

I straightened to my full height and stared down at her. "Pretty sure that's between you and Puck."

Cressida's jaw worked back and forth. "He won't let me back in if you're not happy about it."

"Cress," Dina said, exhaustion in her voice. "You know exactly what you have to do. So, stop playing dumb. Apologize and move on with your life. You were a bitch to the wrong person."

The redhead's cheeks bloomed a deeper red. "It was an accident. But whatever. I'm sorry I *accidentally* spilled a drink on you."

I couldn't help the laugh that broke free at the ridiculous non-apology.

Cressida's eyes narrowed on me. "What? It's not good enough for you?"

"I don't give a damn about your apology. You're welcome back in the bar as long as you don't cause trouble or make Puck feel uncomfortable. I think he's made it clear where you two stand."

That redness crept down Cressida's neck. "What's between Puck and me is none of your business."

"Actually," Dina cut in, "it's very much her business. Don't play stupid. You've seen the way Puck looks at her. The way they *all* look at her."

"All?" Cressida squeaked.

I rolled my lips over my teeth to keep from smiling. Gods, I loved Dina.

Cressida's gaze ping-ponged back and forth between Dina and me. "Disgusting," she spat and then stalked off back to wherever she'd come from.

"Ah, jealousy," Dina muttered.

This time, I didn't try to hold in my laugh or smile. "You're the best."

"And don't I know it."

We finished loading up the cardboard, downed some delicious cupcakes, and got back to work. The lunch rush was a little heavier today. With Puck having the day off, Dina and I switched back and forth between working the tables and the bar.

Amos and Ginger were back, splitting a cheeseburger and the club sandwich with added avocado. Juan was in with a couple of buddies from work. And there were some new faces I pegged as tourists.

"What's the verdict?" I asked as I stopped by Amos and Ginger's table. "Who won today?"

Ginger beamed up at me. "I smoked him. Extra avocado for the win."

She held out a hand, and I gave her a high five.

Amos just shook his head, affection clear on his face. "We're going for the brownie sundae for dessert. That's the trump card."

"That it is," I said with a grin. "I'll get that right in for you."

I walked the order to the pass-through window and then moved to check in with Dina. "You good?"

"Let's swap," she suggested. "I'm getting twitchy."

Dina hated standing still for any length of time.

I grinned at her. "Not enough midday booze hounds for you?"

"Apparently not."

"I got it. I'll refill condiments while you work tables." It was something I could do while keeping an eye on the bar.

"Sounds good." Dina was already off, making the rounds to check on people and chat about local spots with tourists.

I pulled out the jumbo bottles of ketchup and mustard and got to work. I didn't mind the quiet tasks. I could let my mind wander and get lost in the meditative nature of it all. Which is exactly what I did, until the sound of a throat clearing jarred me from my thoughts.

I started to turn, catching the scent before I saw the person.

Wolf. And a wolf I knew. One I hated with every fiber of my being.

There he sat on the stool, easy, casual. His hair was grayer now, but the slope of his nose was so similar to mine.

"Hello, Little Flower. I've missed you."

CHAPTER TWENTY-TWO

Wren

My heart hammered against my ribs. I'd braced for this moment since I'd escaped Red River. I'd trained for it, run through countless scenarios. But nothing had prepared me for this.

I'd expected a snatch-and-grab or an all-out assault. But here was Bastian Boudreaux, sitting at the bar like he didn't have a care in the world. Like he hadn't murdered my mother or tortured me for years on end.

"You look surprised to see me, Fleur."

The use of my birth name had me wincing, a reminder of the endless lashes, broken bones, and burns. But I didn't let myself drop my gaze. If I gave Bastian that submission, it would mean letting him know he'd won.

"You're not welcome here," I ground out, my fingers dropping to my pocket to pull my blade.

"I wouldn't do that if I were you," Bastian cooed. "So many

breakable humans around. You seem especially fond of that elderly couple. Maybe I'll start with them. Rip out their jugulars before you can even retrieve whatever's in your pocket."

My mouth went dry, and my fingers stilled. He would do it, too. Bastian had no regard for human or supernatural life. The only thing he cared about was *more*. More money. More power. More beings under his will.

"That's better," Bastian said, easing back on the stool. "It's good to see you've found some of that fight. It'll be all the more fun to break you all over again."

My hands fisted at my sides as my wolf snarled. My fingernails lengthened to claws, pricking my palms. I focused on the flicker of pain, anything to keep myself from shifting.

Bastian was truly evil. The few times my empath shields had wavered around him, the inky blackness of his soul had nearly drowned me. It was the kind of evil without a cure. The only answer was for it to be snuffed out altogether. But that wouldn't be easy.

"What? No greeting for your old man? No hug?" Bastian challenged, his eyes twinkling.

"The only hug you're getting is a blade between the ribs," I snarled.

His brown eyes sparked gold. "You could try, Little Flower. But you'd fail. Fail because you're so goddamned weak. A stain on my name."

I lifted my chin and still didn't look away. "If you haven't noticed, I don't carry your name. I don't want a damn thing to do with you."

Bastian's jaw worked back and forth as a hint of his anger sparked in his expression. "You never showed me the proper respect, you little slut. You should be bowing to kiss my feet. Grateful I didn't slice your throat the second I took you in. A bastard hybrid," he spat.

Fury swept through me in hot waves. Bastian had always hated that my mother was a caster. Never mind the fact that he was the one who'd slept with her. Apparently, other species were fine to warm his bed but not to bear his young.

Maybe it was his rage at not being able to have another child. He'd certainly tried. Almost every woman in Red River had been forced to try to give him a *true* heir. They'd all failed.

I glared at the man in front of me. "It's not my fault your sperm is weak. That it took the magic in my mother's womb for a child to take hold."

Bastian bared his teeth at me, his canines lengthening. "You'll pay for that. Pay in blood and flesh. Your child will be my heir. Marcelle can't wait."

Bile surged up my throat. My father's beta was possibly more twisted than him. His joy at inflicting pain was unparalleled, and at least half the scars on my body were thanks to him.

"No." Even though my body trembled at the fear and memory taking hold, my voice didn't shake.

Bastian's brown eyes went pure gold, the alpha assuming control. "What did you say to me?"

It was a word I'd never uttered in his presence before, and certainly not in response to the beast himself.

"No." There was a finality in the single syllable. A defiance I'd needed to own for so long.

"You *dare* to defy me?" Bastian's voice made the silverware on the bar top rattle.

"I. Don't. Belong. To. You."

Anger hit me in brutal waves, the emotion raking across my shields in painful slashes. And then there was something more. Bastian's alpha power. It blazed out of him, nearly making my knees buckle.

"You will submit," he growled.

I gripped the edge of the bar, trying to keep myself upright.

"You will come with me and do exactly as I say, or I will dismantle your life, piece by piece. I will slaughter every being who has given you a kind word. And I'll save the worst for those bastard wolves who gave you sanctuary."

A whimper left my lips, and pain spiked through my skull—the price of trying to fight off Bastian's alpha authority. I felt a trickle of blood from my nose and knew I was losing.

"Submit," he snarled.

Then, a new voice joined his. It was familiar but darker than I'd ever heard it before. "The hell she will."

CHAPTER TWENTY-THREE

Ender

I wanted to kill him. No, killing wasn't enough. I wanted to keep Bastian Boudreaux alive while I removed every finger and toe, castrated him, and then moved on to his organs.

I could feel the alpha power coming off him in waves and how he was trying to use it to force Wren's submission. But she wasn't giving in. Holy hell, she was fierce. Still standing, even though her nose bled and her skull likely felt as if it were being crushed.

Just knowing that made me respect her more. The doubts I had about her, the speculation that it all might be some ruse to take us in and make us bow to her father's whims, were melting away day by day. And in place of those doubts came admiration and so much damn regret.

But right now, one thing overrode it all.

Fury.

My blade moved to my hand as if it were a part of me. And in many ways, it was. I pressed the steel tip to a spot just below

Bastian's left shoulder blade. I knew the angle well. One swift strike and the blade would pierce his heart.

I wanted him to suffer so much more than that, though. He deserved the worst this world had to offer. But I would do whatever it took to stop him right now. Even with a room full of witnesses.

"Turn it off," I growled.

The alpha waves ceased as Bastian straightened. He cast a look over his shoulder, a grin tugging at his lips. "You grew up good, boy, despite not having a single family member to raise you."

My canines pressed against my gums, wanting to lengthen. My wolf demanded that we tear out this beast's throat and drown in the taste of his blood.

"I made my own family," I gritted out.

Bastian's brown eyes flashed gold. "Then I guess I'll have to steal them from you, too. A worse fate this time, I think."

My fingers itched to plunge the knife into Bastian's heart, to end him. But out of the corner of my eye, I saw Sheriff Archer eating with two of his deputies. Landing in jail would end my wolf. He wouldn't be able to take captivity.

Bastian laughed, scooting off the stool and away from my knife. "So impotent. Just like all those years ago."

"You have no idea what you've started. But you'll pay in blood," I snarled.

He made a tsking noise. "Be careful, pup. I might take that as a threat. And you know what I do to my enemies."

Wren made a soft, keening noise as if memories were hitting her like a barrage of bullets.

Bastian grinned, evident joy filling him at her pain. "I'll be seeing you, Little Flower."

Wren almost went down then, her legs buckling. She barely caught herself on the edge of the bar. I was already moving, closing the distance. I caught her easily, and with my shifter strength, she felt like nothing more than Princess.

"Easy," I whispered.

Wren didn't say a word. Her eyes had gone glassy and unfocused as if she weren't seeing what was actually in front of her.

I cursed, wrapping an arm around her waist. "Come on. You're all right. I've got you."

I helped her out from behind the bar, moving slowly. The urge to simply pick her up was strong, but I knew what a scene that would make. Dina had already registered that something was wrong. She wove through the tables and met us at the end of the bar. "What's wrong? Who was that man?"

"Space," I gritted out. "Give us a little space."

Anger flashed in Dina's expression, but she nodded. "Take her to the office. I've got the bar."

I lifted my chin in ascent and maneuvered Wren toward the hallway. The moment we were out of view of the patrons, I lifted her into my arms. The fact that Wren didn't protest told me how far gone she was.

The scent of wildflowers and rain filled my nose, and the feeling of home wrapped around me. It was pure temptation and torture all at once.

Shoving open the door to Puck's office, I slid inside and kicked it closed behind me. I lowered us to the couch, half of it laden with random hoodies and paperwork. Puck was such a slob. But none of that mattered now. All that mattered was Wren.

My hand slid up and down her back. "You're okay. You're safe."

She shuddered against me as if some invisible battle raged within her. I wasn't sure how long it took before she spoke. But when she finally did, her words were the last thing I expected.

"Kill me," Wren whispered. "It'd be a mercy."

CHAPTER TWENTY-FOUR

Wren

K*ILL ME. IT'D BE A MERCY.*"

My own words echoed in my ears, but the more they did, the more I was certain it was the path forward. The only way. At least with that, my death would be my choice. Ender might be a monster to some, but I felt confident he would make my death quick.

It would keep the Arcane pack safe, too. If he knew I was gone, my father might simply move on.

Ender pulled back, his amber eyes darkening. "Now, where's the fun in that? There's no challenge if you don't fight back."

There was humor in his words but rage in his eyes. The juxtaposition was potent. Just like the scent of cinnamon and cloves swirling around me. I'd never been this close to Ender or touched this much of him.

I wasn't sure if it was the shock of seeing my father after all these years, hearing his threats, or the feeling of Ender holding me that had me dizzy. All I knew was I wanted to fade into the assassin's calming scent. Disappear into that earthy, heady aroma.

"I'm tired," I whispered.

Ender's expression softened into something I'd never seen before. His fingers slid into my hair and held on. "I know."

"I can't go back. I won't give him that power."

A muscle in Ender's jaw popped. "You will never go back."

I wished I could believe that vow. "You don't know him. Not really. He'll never stop. I betrayed him, and he won't stand for that."

"Maybe not, but *I* don't stand for anyone hurting the people I care about. We've flushed him out. Got him away from the protection of his pack and territory. This is where *we* have the upper hand."

Gods, I wanted that to be true. Wanted us to be able to take out Bastian and all the high-level Red River wolves. I wanted to free not just myself but everyone who had been under Bastian's thumb.

"He won't be here alone," I warned. "He never travels without protection."

"I know," Ender growled. "I saw two unfamiliar wolves in town and knew something was off."

I shuddered, wondering if one of them had been Marcelle.

Ender stiffened beneath me, feeling my tremble. "What did he say to you?"

"It doesn't matter," I mumbled.

"Tell. Me. What. He. Said."

I let out a long breath. "He promised to break me. Torture me all over again. Give me to his beta so I can birth my father's true heir." But that child would still be part caster. It would still be part of *me*. I was just sure Bastian thought he could control them if he had custody of them from birth.

The snarl that tore through the air had my wolf howling. Fur rippled over Ender's arms as he struggled to control his wolf.

It was likely the mating bond that spurred the reaction. Ender wouldn't have any say over those protective instincts.

He took several ragged breaths, pulled himself together, and then finally met my gaze, his eyes pure wolf. "I need to know what happened to you."

I shook my head. "Even if I felt like taking a trip down Fucked-Up Memory Lane, it's not a good idea. You're too on edge."

Not to mention that he'd likely accuse me of lying even if I did tell him. Ender couldn't reconcile the fact that I might be as much of a victim as he was when it came to Bastian's cruelty. And I wasn't sure I had it in me to fight the battle anymore. I wasn't going to try to convince Ender that I wasn't a liar or a con woman out to get him and his pack.

Ender's fingers tightened in my hair, but his thumb was featherlight as it traced the scar on my cheek. "I need to know. To understand. I just... My wolf and my human side are at war, and I need to know the truth. Please."

My eyes flared as I stared back at him, understanding what he was truly asking for. Mates could share memories with each other if they opened their minds. It took a lot of trust, and for me, the cost would be agony—I'd have to let down my empath shields to do it.

My wolf gave me a stern nudge. She wanted me to share, sensed it was the only way.

Fear and anxiety clawed at me as I stared at Ender, his massive body wrapped around mine. "There's no going back."

This wouldn't be us cementing the bond because that would take a claiming mate-bond mark—a bite that would tether us for all eternity. In this life and the next.

But sharing memories like this *would* bring us closer and mean that walking away from each other would be even harder.

I still found myself wanting to give Ender what he'd asked for. Wanting him to know the truth.

I placed my hands on either side of his face, both of us with skin-to-skin contact now, and lowered my shields.

Pain hit me in hot, fiery waves. Anger and fear. Anxiety and the tiniest flicker of hope. But swirling around it all was confusion and doubt.

I tried to ignore the agony of Ender's emotions and opened my mind to him. I let the memories flow and just hoped like hell I wasn't making the biggest mistake of my life.

CHAPTER TWENTY-FIVE

Ender

I didn't feel or see anything at first. But then again, I had no idea *what* to expect. This sort of thing was only possible between mates, so it wasn't as if I'd experienced it before.

Mates.

Just thinking the word had my entire body tightening, but my wolf howled in agreement of the word. He wanted Wren in every way possible. It was my human half that fought it.

A buzz lit my cheeks, in only the places Wren touched me. It was as if a foreign energy emanated from her and seeped into me, my entire form waking up and standing at attention.

Then it began.

The pain.

So much I could barely breathe. And the memories weren't linear. Instead, they were a jumble of snapshots and didn't always make complete sense. But they had a single through line.

Agony.

Blades cutting into Wren's flesh. Whips slicing her open. Freezing cold and wearing nothing but shorts and a tank top as she screamed from the bottom of a dark pit. Branding irons pressed into her flesh. Vicious taunts. Hunger pains.

I was about to cry out for Wren to release me when I heard Bastian's voice in her memory. Cruel and cold. No emotion at all.

"No one escapes me, Little Flower. No one. Look what happened to your mother." A sick chuckle echoed in the dark pit. "Sliced her open in the most painful ways imaginable because she took from me. Tried to steal what was mine. I'll do the same to you if you ever *dream of trying to leave."*

But she had left. Wren had run despite the hovering fear of what might come. She was the strongest person I'd ever known.

I jerked back, the contact with Wren dropping away and taking the memories with it. I stared at the woman on my lap, a different sort of agony taking root now.

Regret.

After everything Wren had been through, I'd only put her through more. I wanted to rip out my heart and give myself all the torture she'd experienced.

I rose, unable to remain still for a single second more. Wren startled as I sat her back on the couch. I stared down at her beautiful face, twisted with what looked like another migraine. It made sense, the emotional overload, the shock of seeing her father. Just more pain I was responsible for.

"I'm sorry." The words felt like barbed wire being yanked from my throat, but it was all I could give her as I turned to stalk out of the room. I nearly ran into Dina, who scowled at me.

"What's going on?" she demanded.

"Stay with her," I ordered. "Don't let her out of your sight. She needs food and Locke's headache tonic. Someone will be back in an hour to get her."

I knew Bastian wouldn't make a move right now. He'd

executed his first play and would wait for our response, hoping we did something stupid. But I still wasn't about to leave Wren alone.

Dina's eyes narrowed. "You do whatever it takes to keep her safe."

"I will," I growled. And for the first time, I truly meant it.

I stalked through the restaurant, patrons reading my mood and swiftly moving out of my way. As I stepped outside, I kept my head on a swivel. My gaze searched for any signs of Red River wolves as I prowled across the parking lots toward Crescent Kingdom.

In my mind? I was with Wren back in that pit. Reliving every ounce of torture she'd endured. I didn't think it would ever stop. And that was exactly what I deserved.

Ripping open the door to the gym, music and the sounds of training hit my ears. I wanted to rip the speakers from the walls and the heavy bags from the ceiling. The urge to destroy was almost more than I could take.

"What the hell are you doing here?" Puck snarled. "You're supposed to be watching Wren."

"Dina's with her," I clipped.

"Dina might be good with a bat, but she won't know what to do if a wolf shifter waltzes into the bar," Puck accused, ripping off his training gloves as the rest of the guys moved in behind him.

King glared at him. "Keep your voices down."

He was right to issue the warning. Plenty of humans were within hearing range.

"Bastian showed. Sat down at the fucking bar."

Snarls surged around me, even with the guys trying to keep their voices low.

"He. Tried. To. Grab. Her?" King gritted out, his fingernails lengthening to claws.

I bit the inside of my cheek so hard I tasted blood. "He tried to force her to submit."

More sounds of derision and anger filled the air. It was the lowest of the low to force a wolf's submission. But it shouldn't have shocked any of us that Bastian would stoop to that level.

"Tell me you got him," Locke pleaded.

My jaw worked back and forth. "I couldn't. The goddamned sheriff was right there, and Wren—she needed me."

Brix's eyes bled to silver. "What. Did. He. Do. To. Her?"

"Threatened her." I couldn't force my mouth to form the details. It was too much. "She got triggered. She...she showed me. Everything he did to her. I—it was so much worse than we could've imagined."

A burn lit in my throat, and pressure built behind my eyes. I couldn't take it. All she'd been through. Our fucking mate. And there was only one thing I knew to do right now. One action I could take to make things better. To atone.

I met each of their gazes. "We can't wait any longer. We have to kill Bastian Boudreaux. Now."

CHAPTER TWENTY-SIX

Wren

THE CREEK BUBBLED AND BABBLED AS IT SWEPT OVER stones and logs and around the fish swimming there without a care in the world. It was peaceful, a sensation opposite of everything coursing through me.

My head still thrummed with the faint echo of a headache, the repercussions of dropping my emotional shields. But it was better than it had been. The tonic and food Dina had given me had helped, along with the dose of caffeine in the form of an iced coffee that King had brought me.

There was something about that tiny gesture. The fact that King registered that moments of heightened emotions could leave me with a migraine eased a little of the hurt he'd caused in my heart. That was King. Quiet actions over words.

I'd wanted to keep working, but the guys refused. Puck said he'd help Dina for the rest of the day, and the other guys took me home. They'd been mostly quiet until we got there, and Locke had offered a movie or a game. I'd said I just needed a little time.

Thankfully, they'd given it to me. Now that the wards were strengthened, and Locke had laid new alarms around the borders, the Arcane territory was safe. At least for now.

Footsteps sounded, then the crack of a twig and crunching dried leaves—someone not trying to hide their approach. I didn't reach for my knife, but when I scented the leather and spice aroma that was only Brix, my muscles eased a fraction.

More relief came as he stepped into view in his wolf form. I wasn't ready for human conversations, but comfort from Brix's animal half? I would take that.

The jet-black wolf slowly sauntered over to me, blue-green eyes assessing and trying to decide if I was open to his approach.

I flipped my hand over in answer, palm up. Brix read the gesture instantly, his steps growing less hesitant. He moved into my space, stepping between my legs and sitting. My hands instantly went to his fur.

My fingers sifted through the softness—the complete opposite of his human half's tough exterior. Brix let out a rumbling sound that almost sounded like a purr.

One corner of my mouth kicked up. "You sound like Princess."

Brix chuffed at that as if to say, "*The hell I do.*"

It only made me grin more.

Brix leaned into me and rested his head on my thigh comfortingly. Gods, it felt good. And I needed it. The simplicity of the gesture, having nothing I needed to explain or talk about...just touch.

We stayed there for a long time, my hands running over his massive, jet-black form as I worked through the days' events. It was like I was an archeologist on a dig, excavating layer after layer.

First came the fear. I had to work through the terror of Bastian knowing where I was, the horror of possibly being back in his clutches. Then came the logistics. How had he found me? Was it Ender's contact? Someone else? If there was a leak in Crescent

Creek, we needed to find it. Finally, the plan. How the hell did I deal with all of this?

Did I need to run? Hide? Start over yet again?

Something told me that's what Bastian expected me to do. And if he'd predicted that, he'd have a plan to go along with it. Likely men at all the routes into and out of town. The bus stations and the nearest airport. He'd hope I'd be stupid enough to venture out alone so he could snag me.

But I wasn't going to play that game. Wouldn't fall into his trap. I'd take my time. Think through all the possibilities.

The dull ache in my head intensified a fraction, and it took me a second to realize it wasn't coming from me but from Brix. His emotions raked at my shields as he rested peacefully against me. The ache spread from my head and went straight to my heart.

I understood why. As triggering as Bastian being in Crescent Creek was for me, it had to be equally so for Brix, just in a different way. His would be rooted in fear and guilt, the responsibility he felt for being unable to save his sister.

My empath gift flared inside me, never wanting another creature to feel emotional pain. My hands continued their ministrations, sifting through his fur. I knew it was dumb, reckless even, but I lowered my shields just a fraction, enough to let in a sliver of Brix's pain.

His emotional wounds slammed into me, trying to widen the opening, but I battled them back. I only allowed a sliver, taking it into me as my hands slid over him in nonsensical patterns. A buzz started in my palms, my gift healing the darkness within him and easing it just a touch.

It wouldn't be enough to change his makeup or mean he would be free of all the demons haunting him. But it was enough to take the edge off and make sure Brix no longer felt like he was drowning.

A rumbling growl slid from Brix's throat. I instantly slammed my shields up again as I pulled my hands back. His wolf form began to vibrate. Bones cracked, and his entire being transformed.

A few seconds later, Brix stood before me in his human form, naked as the day he was born but seeming completely unbothered by it. He glared at me, his eyes flashing. He didn't speak right away, but the entire world slipped out from under me when he did.

"You're an empath."

CHAPTER TWENTY-SEVEN

Brix

I STARED DOWN AT THE WOMAN BEFORE ME, MY MATE, THE miracle of a being only growing more wondrous with every moment that revealed yet another of her secrets.

An empath.

It shouldn't have been possible. They were said to be extinct. The last known empath had been killed a generation ago, her gift bled dry, her life along with it.

Emotions warred within me—fear, wonder, anger, amazement—and the unfamiliar sensations had my wolf snarling.

Wren frantically shook her head. "I'm not. Why would you say that?"

My eyes narrowed. "You are. I felt something the first time you touched me in my wolf form and couldn't identify it. But this time? I felt you easing the darkness. You bled it out of me."

All color drained from Wren's face as panic took root. "You're mistaken. I—"

I grabbed her wrist and pulled her to me as I struggled to keep my hold on her gentle. "You're my *mate.* Do you honestly think I would betray you by telling this secret to the world?"

So many pieces slid into place. All the ways Wren was guarded. Her headaches. Her reaction when emotions ran high.

"Brix," she whispered.

"Trust me," I begged. It was the ultimate request. I knew I had no right to that gift, but I asked for it anyway. "Trust me to protect you in every way I can."

A little of the fear slid out of Wren's expression, her face softening as she looked up at me. "If anyone finds out..."

"I know." I pulled her against me and wrapped her in my arms as if I could shield her from everything that could possibly come her way.

She shuddered against me but burrowed in. The action was more of a gift than she'd ever know.

My fingers tangled in her hair, stroking the same way she had with my fur. "When did you know?"

Wren was quiet for a moment before speaking. "I'm not sure. I've just *known* for as far back as I can remember. My mom said she could feel it even when I was a baby. She had to learn to shield her emotions from me because I'd often try to heal her when she was in distress."

I pulled back and brushed the hair away from her face. "She could shield?"

Wren nodded. "Through her caster magic. She tried to shield me, too, so no one would find out, but I burned through the spells too quickly. That's when she knew she had to run. Because she understood what my father would do if he found out."

A low growl tore from my throat. If Bastian knew what his daughter was, he would've used every last ounce of her power. People paid top dollar for healings. And with how rare empaths and their emotional healings were, they would've paid a fortune. "She hid you."

"We moved around a ton. Never stayed in one place for more than a few months. As I got older, she taught me how to shield myself—both my empath gifts and my shifter nature. With my unique eyes, I had to learn to conceal every other piece of myself if we had any hope of staying hidden."

But they hadn't stayed hidden forever. Ender had shared some of what he'd seen while in Wren's mind, including the fact that Bastian had killed her mother when she was quite young.

"How did he find you?" I asked.

Wren let out a long breath, grief sweeping through her beautiful turquoise eyes. "I still don't know. He has sources everywhere. Maybe my scent shields slipped at some point and a supernatural caught my smell. Maybe a human saw a photo of me and put two and two together."

The grief in her expression transformed into anger, hot pulses of it washing over her beautiful face. "He liked me to be in the dark. To never know how he got to us or how he knew certain things. I'm fairly confident someone who wields dark magic is on his payroll."

I gnashed my back teeth as I struggled to maintain my composure. Bastian had tortured Wren in so many ways outside of the physical. And the emotional wounds might be the worst.

My lips skimmed her forehead. "I'm so sorry, Little Warrior. So damn sorry."

The nickname King had bestowed on her was more accurate than he could know. Wren was a fighter through and through. Battling to make her way out of hell and warring to get to us, where she was always meant to be.

"I'm just so tired," she whispered. "Tired of running. Fighting. I just want it to be done."

I heard the defeat in her voice and understood it. She'd been fighting for her entire life. Never free to simply...be. She deserved that freedom, a life without worry or fear. And I would do anything to give it to her.

"Wren." My thumb traced her jawline. "Why do you think the universe brought you to us?"

She looked up at me, her brows pulling together.

"So you can rest. Let us fight for you. Let us give you strength. None of us is as powerful alone as we are together."

Wren's eyes glistened, her unshed tears glittering in the fading light of the day. "Brix."

She needed more than my words. She needed my actions.

I let my hands fall from her face and took a step back before dropping to my knee and dipping my head to look at the ground. "Wren. Little Warrior. Mate. I swear my devotion to you and only you. Where you lead, I will follow. What you need, I will provide. My life is yours to do with as you will."

CHAPTER TWENTY-EIGHT

Wren

I STARED DOWN AT THE MAN BEFORE ME. HIS DARK HAIR FELL over his face, and his tan skin glowed in the fading light. Brix was an alpha. He had the power to lead a pack. Yet here he was, kneeling before me as a submissive.

This was a pledge of fealty. A sacred oath. To me. *For* me.

"Brix," I croaked.

He raised his head slowly until those captivating blue-green eyes met mine. "I love you, Wren. My life is yours."

A tear slid free, trailing down my cheek and falling to the earth. Brix pushed to his feet, his hands framing my face to wipe away the tears. "I love you. I didn't think I was capable of it, but you showed me differently. You showed me I can still come alive, even if it hurts."

"Brix." I could only manage to say his name, but maybe that said it all.

He leaned into me, his mouth taking mine in a slow kiss. He'd given me the words, but his kiss said more. Everything that was beyond language poured into the connection, his lips on mine, his tongue stroking in. He coaxed and teased, toyed and tempted.

And when Brix pulled back, he left me breathless. He searched my face, seeming as if he were trying to find something. "Let me make you mine. Let me be wholly yours."

Emotion caught in my throat, a tangle of countless things making it hard to speak or even breathe. Because I knew what he meant. The mating bond. The commitment that would seal us together in this life and the next.

"Yes." My mouth spoke the word before my brain even registered it.

It was all Brix needed. He dropped his hands to the hem of my tee and lifted it up and over, letting it flutter to the forest floor. Then he deftly unfastened my bra, letting that fall, too.

He cupped my breasts, his head dropping for a moment to pull a bud into his mouth. My back arched, moving me into Brix, closer to his touch, closer to everything.

Brix sucked deeply, making heat and wetness gather between my thighs. I could smell his need and desire mixing with mine, stirring together in something that was only ours.

As he worked my nipple with his tongue, his fingers moved to the button of my jeans. Suddenly, his mouth was gone, and he was sliding my pants and underwear down my legs as he dropped to his knees again. He skimmed his knuckles over my thighs, and I shuddered, that want inside me flaring brighter.

"My little warrior, so beautiful in the twilight. Like it was made to caress your skin."

I sucked in a breath, words escaping me as I stared down at the beautiful man before me. His beauty was not just in the golden skin pulled taut over toned muscle or even the hypnotic blue-green eyes. It was so much more. It was in all he was to me. All he had given me.

Brix pulled off one sneaker and then the other. In a flash, my jeans were gone, too. Suddenly, I was just as bare as he was. Brix stood, his big body pressed to mine, moving me backward until I hit a tree.

My breaths came in quick pants as Brix's lips skimmed my neck and his fingers slid between my thighs. "Where should I bite you, Little Warrior?" Those fingers spread me open and delved into my heat. "Somewhere for the world to see?" He nipped my neck. "Or somewhere only for us?" His head dipped lower so he could lightly bite my breast.

My nipples hardened to painful points and I nearly cried out for release, for Brix. I arched into him, moving my core against his hand.

Brix's head jerked back, his eyes bleeding silver. "In a hurry, mate?"

"Yes," I breathed.

"Let's see what we can do about that…"

Brix's fingers were gone, and without warning, he thrust into me. My mouth fell open as my head tipped back, bracing itself against the tree. The stretch and the pressure were everything I needed, everything I wanted.

He pulled out only to slam into me again, the move somehow managing to be brutal and gentle all at once—brutal in its sheer power and gentle, with Brix knowing exactly what I needed.

My fingers dug into his back, claws lengthening and pressing into his flesh.

Brix let out a snarl of pleasure. "Mark me, mate. I want to carry your brands with me into forever."

My hips bucked against him at those words, my wolf letting out a howl. She'd wanted this for so long, craved it. My teeth pressed against my gums as saliva pooled in my mouth. Everything rode me to bite, to claim, to belong to Brix for eternity.

He powered into me, my inner walls quaking from the force. Every part of me trembled, anticipation and pleasure coursing through me. But I wanted more of him. No, I wanted everything: his seed, his bite, his brand.

"Brix," I rasped. "Take me."

The growl that tore through the air had a power I'd never heard before. He thrust, going impossibly deeper, his movements picking up speed to a fevered pace. Brix lifted his head, his canines lengthening. Mine did the same in response. His eyes were pure silver as they met mine. "Forever," he snarled.

"Forever," I echoed.

Brix slammed into me so deeply that it was its own brand. His teeth clamped down on my shoulder as I mirrored the gesture on him. The pleasure that swept through me was unlike anything I'd ever known. It rode the line between agony and ecstasy, each one driving the other higher.

My walls clamped down around Brix as he emptied into me, and I took it all. Every ounce of pleasure and pain. Because it was him, us. Everything we were together.

We rode every wave until our bodies quieted. Brix pulled his teeth from my shoulder and licked the brand. I shuddered with the sensation of it, trying to breathe deeply and bring myself back under control.

When I did, I took in the mark. It was to the side of his teeth marks. A totem that would present itself on Brix, too—a matching set that would only be ours. It looked like a tattoo but the dark, ink-like substance shimmered slightly in the dark. It was a heart with a knife through it. Pleasure and pain.

Brix cupped my face. "Because you made me feel again. Made me know I was seen."

"I love you," I whispered against his lips as he slid from my body.

"More than life," he rasped.

Then Brix took me to the creek. He cleaned me, dried me with a towel they had stored in one of the trees, and then dressed me as if I were the most precious thing in the world to him. Because I was. Just like he was to me.

He kissed me again. This time when he pulled back, something passed over those beautiful eyes.

A trickle of fear slid through me. "What?"

Brix pulled me to him and held me tightly. "Don't make me keep this secret from my brothers."

I knew what he meant. The bond told me. He didn't want to shoulder the knowledge of my empath status alone. But the idea of telling all of them terrified me.

Calming, reassuring feelings trickled through our bond as Brix tried to reassure me. "I'll be with you the whole time."

I pulled back and met his gaze. Trust. I had to give him that. So, I said the only word I could.

"Okay."

CHAPTER TWENTY-NINE

Wren

BLOOD ROARED IN MY EARS IN A CROSS BETWEEN POUNDING ocean waves and staccato percussion. Brix had sent a mind link message to the rest of the pack, asking them to meet us in the living room. I knew it was the right thing to do, the honorable one. It wasn't fair to make Brix keep this sort of secret. And if I truly wanted a bond with these men, I needed to be honest about who I really was. Give them all of me.

But just because it was the right thing didn't mean I wasn't terrified beyond measure. Brix's fingers slid through mine, squeezing gently. His reassuring presence calmed me a fraction, but not nearly as much as it typically would have. Too much was at stake.

I was no longer afraid that one of the guys would sell me out to the highest bidder, but I had plenty of other fears. That they would be angry I'd kept this secret from them. That I'd somehow used the gift to manipulate them. That I was an abomination.

Nausea churned in my belly, acid and fear mixing in a brutal stew. It was more than I could take.

Brix gripped my hand tighter as we moved inside, heading toward the faint sounds of voices. He led me through the maze of hallways and into the living room. The moment we stepped inside, all talking ceased. Four sets of eyes snapped to the two of us.

Kingston's nostrils flared, scenting what I was sure was a mixture of sex and something else, something deeper. "You've bonded."

A smile spread across Locke's face, but he didn't move from his spot on the couch, knowing Brix's wolf would be a bit territorial at the moment. "Congratulations. Both of you. This is amazing."

Puck's lips twitched. "I can smell you on our mate, but if you truly pleased her, why does she look so nervous?"

He was teasing Brix, giving him a brotherly ribbing, but it only served to increase my anxiety. Brix dropped my hand, but only so he could wrap his arm around my shoulders and pull me into his side.

"It's something else." Ender's eyes narrowed, his gaze sweeping over me. It wasn't aggressive or harsh but it was an assessment.

Kingston instantly straightened. "What's wrong? Did something happen? Is Wren—?"

Brix held up a hand to silence him. Kingston's eyes flashed, his alpha nature not especially liking being told to shut up. Brix looked down at me in question.

I shook my head slightly. "You tell them. I can't."

I couldn't get my mouth to form the words: *I'm an empath.* It felt far too terrifying, even in a place I felt the safest.

Brix's thumb skated up and down my arm as he scanned the room. "Wren is an empath."

It was a single sentence, but it might as well have been a bomb. The room went eerily silent as if everybody had been stunned by the blast and were still trying to get their bearings.

King managed to speak first. "How?" he croaked.

Puck gave a slight shake of his head. "They're extinct."

"It's not possible," Ender said as he shoved to his feet, moving to pace.

Locke looked at me with reverence. "The headaches. They happen when you're emotionally overloaded."

I nodded, biting my lip before speaking. "If my shields drop or if there's too much feeling in a confined space."

"The Lair the other day... We were all so pissed off. That's why you opened the door," King surmised.

"Yes." I glanced at Puck. "And that first day we met. You startled me, and my shields faltered. So, when you touched me, I felt everything you did. All the pain you were hiding from the world. Everything."

Puck stared back at me, not even blinking.

"I don't know what causes the emotions," I hurried to say. "So, it's not like I'm invading your memories or can read minds."

"You don't have to worry about that," Puck said quietly. "I wouldn't care if you *could* read my mind."

Air left my lungs in a whoosh, relief sweeping through me.

"It's incredible. A gift," Kingston breathed as Locke nodded.

But Ender kept on pacing, his jaw working back and forth. I waited, giving him time to work through whatever he needed to. Finally, his footsteps slowed, and he turned to face me. "I just...I don't know how it's possible. Even the lore we used to hear. It all just seems like a tale from a storybook."

My gaze flicked up to Brix, and he nodded. The only reason Brix had believed was because he'd felt it. I needed to give the same to Ender.

I slipped out from under Brix's arm, feeling the loss instantly. But I kept going, moving toward Ender. The assassin eyed me warily, and I didn't blame him. I stopped a few feet from him, my hands at my sides. "Can I show you?"

Ender blinked at me, uncertainty swirling in his expression. "Will it change me?"

I shook my head. "I can't do much. If I do, it has the power to take me under."

Locke and Puck were immediately on their feet. "No," Puck ordered. "Don't do anything that will put you in danger."

"It's not worth the risk," Locke added.

"I know my limits, and I know them well. A little healing just makes me tired and sometimes gives me a headache. That's it," I told them.

Locke shook his head. "I don't—"

"Please," I whispered. "I need to do this."

I needed Ender to believe. I needed all of them to see.

Locke snapped his mouth closed, and I turned back to Ender, holding up my hands. "May I?"

More of that wariness clouded Ender's amber eyes. "Okay."

I didn't wait. Didn't want to give him a chance to change his mind. I placed my hands on his cheeks the way I had in Puck's office earlier today. Ender's scruff bit into my palms, but I relished the feeling as I focused.

Carefully, I lowered my emotional shields, inch by inch. At the slightest crack, darkness poured into me. Agony from all Ender had lived through. Guilt.

I pushed back, not letting more in but taking the darkness into me, swallowing it whole. It swirled through me as I let my light battle it. My head pounded, and my flesh burned as invisible claws of emotion raked through my mind.

"It's too much," Kingston snarled. "It's hurting her."

I dropped my hands, knowing I had to break the connection or risk doing real damage to myself. I stumbled back, and King caught me.

Ender stared at me in wonder. "It's true. I-I've never felt anything like it."

Kingston steadied me. "Are you all right?"

I nodded quickly. "I'm fine. I just… I'll need a little rest."

"I can get you the headache tonic," Locke said, moving to head out of the room.

But King stopped him. "Wait." His gaze roamed over me. "Who knows?"

I swallowed hard. "My mom did. But she's gone. So, only the five of you."

Ender cursed. "You've been living with this alone?"

"I had no choice. You know what would have happened to me if someone found out."

King gripped my shoulders as if I might disappear right in front of him. "The whole world would hunt you. Not just the wolves. Not only the supernaturals. Everyone."

CHAPTER THIRTY

Kingston

I paced my office as Locke laid out the new additions to our security. Motion sensors. An electric border fence that would fry anyone with human or supernatural code in their DNA unless they were wearing a special token that deactivated the invisible barrier. More cameras.

There was always paid security personnel, but that introduced the risk of someone turning on us. And the only people I truly trusted were those in the house.

"I think that's enough to start," Puck said, fatigue thick in his voice.

I knew why. It was two in the morning, and we were all running on empty. Our pack had been hit by one thing after another, and we needed to recover. The only silver lining was that Wren was currently passed out in bed.

Locke had given her a headache tonic while Puck made her dinner. After eating and drinking, she'd gone straight to sleep. We'd all watched over her for longer than we should've before leaving her in Brix's care and moving on to plan.

Ender let out a low growl. "I'm not sure it's enough."

I turned to him. "It'll never be enough. But it's a start. Though if we don't get some rest, none of us will be of any use in protecting her."

I knew I'd gotten through to him when Ender's shoulders slumped, but he lifted his head in assent. "I'll see you all in the morning." He stalked out of the room before we could say a word.

"I ordered the tech. It should be here tomorrow or the next day," Locke said, rolling up his plans.

It felt like a million and one things could change between now and then—an infinite number of horrible things. But I shoved every last one from my mind. "Thank you," I said, easing into the chair behind my desk.

As Locke headed for the door, Puck didn't move to leave. I could feel his eyes on me. He might be the jokester of the group, but that façade hid his astute nature. He saw far more than those around him would believe.

Finally, I met Puck's green gaze but didn't speak; I simply waited.

"You gonna be able to hold it together?" he asked.

"I don't know," I answered honestly.

Surprise flitted across Puck's expression. "I didn't think you'd give me the truth."

"What good would a lie do any of us? We're all a wreck and know it because we can feel it through the pack bonds."

The link allowed us to snatch echoes of each other's emotions. It was nothing like what Wren could do, but it meant it was useless to lie about how you were feeling.

Puck stared at me for a long moment. "What do you need?"

It was a kindness, that question. But he couldn't give me what I really needed: Wren's safety and forgiveness.

"You're doing it." That wasn't a lie. Puck was doing everything he could to help me. To help us.

His mouth flattened into a thin line, but he nodded. "Don't stay in here torturing yourself for too long."

Puck knew me too well.

"Good night," I said, fatigue swirling around the two words.

"Night," Puck echoed, heading for the door.

I stared through the open doorway for a long time before leaning back in my chair. My head tipped back until all I saw was the ceiling. My office had intricate designs in the plasterwork up there: a geometric design I could trace for hours. And that was good because I had a feeling sleep wouldn't be finding me anytime soon.

The faint sound of footsteps caught my attention. They were light. Bare feet. A slight figure. By the time the mystery individual reached my office, I'd straightened. Just in time to see Wren reach my doorway.

Her hair hung around her in a tangle of waves matted from sleep. She wore an oversized shirt I was pretty sure belonged to Puck, her bare legs peeking out from beneath it. She was fucking gorgeous. Had the kind of beauty that froze a man to the spot, punched through his chest, grabbed his heart in a vicious fist, and clung to it tightly.

"Are you okay?" I croaked.

It was a stupid question. Of course, she wasn't. But I had to ask.

She nodded. "Headache's gone."

"Good."

Wren didn't move. Not to leave. Not to come closer. And wasn't that a metaphor for where we stood? Hovering on the threshold of what we both wanted.

"Do you need something?" I rasped.

She bit her bottom lip, making my jeans suddenly feel two sizes tighter. She released that hold and let out a breath, stepping inside. "I wanted to see how you were doing."

I stared at the beautiful woman in front of me—so raw and real and everything I'd ever wanted. Holding our cards close to our chests had done nothing but hurt us. So, I decided to give her my brutal truth. No self-protection, no shielding, just me.

"Not good," I croaked. "I miss you. I'm fucking terrified that something's going to happen to you and it'll all be my fault. I'm scared you'll never forgive me for not having your back when you needed me the most. I'm worried I can't be the leader my pack needs me to be. That I'll make the wrong decision or not give my brothers what they need."

I sucked in a sharp breath. "And having Bastian in Crescent Creek has all these memories of my sister flooding me. It's killing me. And knowing that he hurt you, too? I want to rip him limb from limb. I'm a wreck, Wren. A shattered mess. And I don't want anyone to know."

CHAPTER THIRTY-ONE

Wren

I stared at the man behind the desk. Some part of my brain recognized him as Kingston, but it was as if he'd completely changed in front of my eyes. King had always been reserved, never sharing too much. So, who was this stranger laying himself bare before me now?

It wasn't easy for an alpha to admit weakness. It was in their DNA to show no mercy and know that every tiny fracture in their façades could be manipulated in battle and lead to their demise.

What Kingston had just done was the equivalent of baring his neck to me. It was a sign of submission and complete trust. And it knocked me sideways.

My breaths came quicker as I took one step and then another, walking toward the man who'd just given me the ultimate gift. I had no idea what to give him in return; I only knew I needed to be closer to do it. When I reached the massive man, I stopped just in front of him, so close I had to step between his legs.

King stared up at me, evident pain and wonder in his gorgeous pale-blue eyes. But he made no move to touch me and didn't ask for anything.

So, I touched him.

My hands lifted and slid through his dark hair. King let out a sound that resembled a purr—deeper than Princess's, but the quality was the same. He slowly bowed his head, lowering until it connected with my belly.

My fingernails scraped his scalp, and that purr morphed into a soft growl. "Too much?" I asked.

"Perfect," King mumbled.

I kept massaging his head as if it would solve all our problems. But I knew it wouldn't. I realized I had to be brave, too.

Sucking in a breath, I gave him a piece of *my* truth. "I'm scared you'll never be able to see past who my father is."

King didn't lift his head, but his hands moved to my hips, holding on as if I were his lifeline. "You're not the man who brought you into this world. I won't even call him your father because he's not. He's the bastard who terrorized you and held you captive, nothing more."

Kingston's grip on me tightened with each sentence, but I took in every ounce of honesty in that touch. My fingers slid lower, kneading King's neck. "His blood is still in me."

"No," King clipped. "It's not. Because you are your own person. You fought everyone who tried to break you and made yourself into a warrior."

A burn lit down my throat as pressure built behind my eyes. "Will you tell me about her? Your sister?"

Kingston stiffened but slowly forced himself to relax. "Natasha. Her name was Natasha."

"Natasha." My mouth formed the syllables as if I were trying to get to know her that way.

"She was a year older than me and so full of mischief and life.

Right up until Bastian's men kidnapped her from a nightclub and put her into their trafficking operation."

Sickness slid through me. I'd heard the enforcers talking about the operation a handful of times, the darkest of the dark things they were involved in, selling women to the highest bidders and throwing them into a life of horrors.

"It took me two years to find her," King rasped. "Two years of hell for her."

My heart thumped against my ribs. I hadn't known Kingston had found his sister. I'd thought my father killed her.

"We got her out of where they were holding her, but she was nothing but skin and bones. And practically catatonic. The only safe way home was to hide out on a damn fishing boat." Kingston paused, his throat working as he tried to swallow. "She threw herself overboard during the night, preferring death to living with the memories of what had happened to her."

Tears tracked down my cheeks, and my hands fisted in King's tee. There were no appropriate words. Nothing that could ease that kind of pain. But I had to try. "I'm so sorry," I croaked. "It's not enough, but it's all I have."

King's head lifted, and I saw pure agony in his eyes. "It's not yours to be sorry for."

"Isn't it?" I asked. "I should've plunged a knife into Bastian's back years ago and taken the death sentence that would've come from it."

Silver sparked in Kingston's gaze. "And then what? His beta would've taken over and continued it all. It would've done nothing but extinguish your light. A light this world needs. A light this *pack* needs."

"And what about you? What do *you* need?"

His hand lifted, his fingers brushing away my fallen tears. "You, Wren. My little warrior. What I've always needed was you."

Fresh tears began to fall, spilling down my cheeks and onto

King's fingers. "I'm scared you'll always see him when you look at me."

Kingston's expression gentled as he gazed up at me. "I see *you*. Your fierceness. Your gentle care. The way you give to those around you, even when they don't deserve it. I see everything about you. And one day, you'll see that, too. But I'm not in a rush."

He stood then, pushing his chair back and towering over me before bending, his lips hovering for a moment before pressing gently to my forehead.

Suddenly, he was gone.

But the feeling of him wasn't.

The place where King had kissed me still burned. It was a scalding brand—a promise of forever.

CHAPTER THIRTY-TWO

Wren

I'M TELLING YOU, SHE WAS INTO ME," JUAN PROTESTED FROM his spot on the stool at Arcane, a burger and fries in front of him as Clyde, Dina, Puck, and Franco looked on.

Franco let out a snort of amused derision. "Dude, she flipped you off as she walked to her car."

Juan just grinned. "She's fiery. Likes to keep me on my toes."

"She's probably going to take out a restraining order," Puck muttered.

Juan glared at him. "You'd know all about that." He turned to me. "Isn't he supposed to stay one hundred yards away from you now?"

I choked on a laugh as I slid Clyde a refill of his Coke.

"Hey," Puck protested, pulling me into his arms. "I'm Birdie's favorite."

I patted his chest. "Of course you are, buddy."

A growl rumbled from his throat. "I'm *not* your buddy."

Franco covered his laugh with a cough. "Caught in the friend zone, huh?"

"I'll show you the friend zone," Puck muttered, tipping me back and taking my mouth with his. His tongue stroked in, that taste of smoky whiskey filling my mouth. I moaned, the world going a little blurry around me.

As Puck straightened us both and pulled his mouth from mine, sounds of hoots and hollers filled the air from various patrons. It was my turn to glare at Puck. "You didn't."

He just grinned at me. "Sometimes, actions speak louder than words."

"You didn't seem like you minded it all that much, girlie," Clyde said, amusement lacing his tone. "If you had, you'd have put that Brit on his ass."

"Hey," Puck protested. "I could take her."

"Keep telling yourself that, boy," Clyde muttered, reaching for his burger.

I couldn't help but giggle. Gods, I loved this crew. And as I filled more drinks for Dina to hand out at the tables, I realized I was glad I hadn't run. Because these people were becoming my family. Not just the guys but also Dina, Clyde, Juan, and Franco. They were giving me something I'd never had before. A home.

As I reached for another tall glass, I caught sight of an envelope beneath it. Frowning at my name scrawled across it, I picked it up and opened it.

These days, I was braced for a threat from Bastian, the remaining Death Walkers, or even the dark mages. But I found something else entirely. I tugged a woven string bracelet from the envelope.

It was six different shades of blue, and as its smell reached my nose, I recognized Kingston's mint and pine scent, along with something else. Magic? I tugged out a piece of paper and scanned it.

I see you, Little Warrior. Blue eyes that melt from one shade to the next. Eyes that take in everything around you. That see more than anyone else. Eyes that make everyone feel seen, too. This bracelet has an enchantment that should help with your headaches. I love you. – King

I struggled to swallow, countless emotions clogging my throat. I couldn't break, not here. But the fact that King had woven this and then took it to someone to imbue it with protective magic meant more than I could say. And that he'd written those three little words? I almost couldn't process it.

"Can I help you put it on?" Puck whispered, his lips grazing my ear.

I turned, searching his green eyes. "You knew he was doing this?"

"He left at three this morning to make it back before we left for work. Asked me to put the note somewhere you'd find it."

Phantom pressure constricted my sternum. "Yes. Will you help me put it on?"

Puck took the bracelet from my hand and tied it around my left wrist. It shimmered faintly in the lights from above, assuring me the magic was there. "He knows he messed up," Puck said softly. "He's trying to make it right."

"I know," I croaked, then looked up at Puck. "I'm scared that he *thinks* he can separate me from Bastian but won't actually be able to."

"He already has," Puck said, certainty lacing his words. "That moment was a shock, but he sees who you really are. He knows it to the depths of his bones. He just needed time to process it all."

Gods, I wanted Puck to be right. I hoped it with everything I had. But the more I got in this life, the more I had to lose. I knew better than most that the things you loved could be torn away from you in infinite ways.

CHAPTER THIRTY-THREE

Wren

Chocolate lava cake with French vanilla ice cream and homemade whipped cream," Puck said, a cocky grin on his face as he handed me the plate.

My stomach growled as I took it and burrowed back into the cushions on the couch in the living room. "This looks like heaven."

"Wait until you taste it," Locke said, grabbing a plate from the tray.

Puck speared him with a dirty look. "I knew one of the cakes was missing from my taste test."

Locke just grinned. "You can't leave chocolate just lying around. You know it's my favorite."

Kingston chuckled as he took a plate, too. "You do know it's his weakness. You gotta guard that stuff with your life."

Princess let out a meow and leapt onto the back of the couch between Ender and me, leaning in to sniff my plate.

"Oh, no. Chocolate is bad for kitties," I said, moving the plate to the side.

Princess meowed again, but this one had a distinctly pissed-off bent to it.

I sent her a warning look. "Be nice."

She headbutted my chin in answer.

"That's better." I scooped up some whipped cream with my finger and held it out to her. "Here you go."

"You spoil her," Ender mumbled.

"And you don't?" I challenged. "You built her a pussy palace. And I caught you singing her a lullaby a couple of days ago."

Ender's cheeks pinked. "She likes that song."

"Don't say pussy," Brix muttered. "It makes me hard, and I really want to enjoy this dessert."

Kingston choked on a bite of cake, and Locke leaned over to pat him on the back. "Who are you kidding? Wren *breathes,* and you get hard."

Brix shrugged. "Fair."

I giggled and ate some cake. The chocolate exploded on my tongue, mixing with the rich ice cream and fluffy whipped cream. I couldn't help the moan that slipped free as my eyes closed. I took my time enjoying the bite. But when my eyes opened again, I found five sets staring at me, all sparking with gold or silver.

Heat flamed in my cheeks. "Sorry. It was really good."

Puck lowered himself to the spot on the other side of me and leaned in to press a kiss to my temple. "Never apologize for enjoying what I make you. Makes me happy as hell."

"Happy and hard," Brix muttered.

I choked on a laugh. "You're welcome?"

He sent me a playful scowl. "You're going to pay for that later."

I stuck out my tongue at him. "It's not a punishment if I enjoy it."

"Jesus," Ender muttered, pushing to his feet. "I need a workout and a cold-ass shower."

"That's because of *your* choices," Puck called after him.

He wasn't wrong, but I couldn't help but wonder what the path forward looked like for Ender and me. So many things had gone wrong for us. And even though he was coming to terms with the truth, there was a lot to repair.

Locke moved as if sensing my mood. He lowered himself to the spot Ender had vacated but pushed in close, wrapping an arm around me. "You guys will figure it out. Promise."

"I hope you're right," I muttered.

Brix stared after Ender for a moment and then pushed to his feet. "I'll go check on him."

Their bond was a close one. Maybe because of the trauma they'd shared as pups. Perhaps because they had the same sort of darkness within them. Whatever it was, I was glad they had each other.

This was how a pack should be: everyone looking out for one another, reading moods and providing support when needed. Just another gift the guys had given me. It was more than family or home; it was something deeper. And I wanted to do whatever I could to hold on to it.

I burrowed into the pillows, Puck at my back and Locke at my front. Brix usually slept with us, too, but he still hadn't returned from checking on Ender. I couldn't deny that his absence put me on edge. Partially because I missed him but also because I worried about Ender.

Puck hooked an arm around my waist and nuzzled my hair. Locke's eyes met mine in the dark, the only light coming from the cracked bathroom door. He slid his fingers through mine and pressed a kiss to my forehead.

I'd never felt safer than I did between them. Cared for.

Cherished. Protected. And because of that security, sleep claimed me before I could even count to ten. But I didn't have that same protection in my dreams. There, I was vulnerable to all sorts of monsters.

Rain pelted down on me, making it hard to see. My body shivered and burned all at the same time. The freezing rain chilled me to the bone, but the slices on my back were pure fire.

"I'll beat the weakness out of you, Fleur. The submission. We will make a real wolf of you yet," Bastian snarled.

The whip cracked, the only warning before a fresh wave of flames ignited across my back. I tried to hold back all sound, knowing it would only make my father angrier. But a soft whimper escaped my lips. A human wouldn't have been able to hear it, but my father wasn't human. He shouldn't even qualify as animal. He was pure monster.

A snarl tore through the air. The whip cracked again, and more fire engulfed my back. It happened over and over until I was no longer standing, held up only by the ties at my wrists.

A figure filled my blurry vision. Not Bastian but his beta, Marcelle. His lip curled. "Weak abomination. Maybe we can beat the caster out of her, too."

The ground trembled, and I knew it was because my father neared. A man who absolutely despised me. His hot breath cascaded over my cheek. "You think they'll save you? They can't get you here. Your pain is mine and mine alone. And the second any of those Arcanes even try to come for you, I'll rip out their still-beating hearts."

A sob tore from my throat as my tears mixed with the rain.

Bastian spat at me. "So damned weak. Ending you would be a mercy to us all. But not until you cower. Not until you bleed."

He pulled out a blade, and the moment it carved into my skin, I screamed.

CHAPTER THIRTY-FOUR

Locke

MY WOLF GROWLED, PUSHING AT MY SKIN, WANTING FREE. When I didn't wake, the growling intensified, and he raked his claws against my insides. It was enough to make my eyelids flutter, the faint glow of the room coming into focus. And that's when I heard it.

A pained whimper.

Every part of me came alert as my gaze focused on the woman in front of me. Wren whimpered again, her face contorting in agony. I knew it had to be a nightmare, but she didn't thrash like you might expect. The only signs that anything was wrong were her voice and the expression on her face.

I reached out a hand and skimmed it over her cheek. "Wren. Wake up. You're safe."

The contact had her striking out, trying to fight me off as Puck jerked awake behind her. I managed to block Wren's blow, catching her wrist. "It's okay. It's just a dream."

"What the hell?" Puck mumbled. But it only took him a matter of seconds to realize what was happening. He held her tightly so she wouldn't hurt herself.

I pressed my forehead to Wren's, wrapping her in my scent and touch, letting her know I was there. "Wake up. We're here. We've got you."

She threw herself hard against Puck's hold, but the action startled her awake. A strangled sound left her throat—more animal than human.

"Hey, hey. It's okay." I framed Wren's face with my hands as Puck eased up on his hold.

"Wha—? Oh, gods. It was so real," she croaked.

Puck released her entirely, pushing up against the pillows. "You're safe, Birdie."

She blinked a few times and moved to sit, pulling her knees into her chest.

I shoved up, too, needing to be close to her. So much pain swirled in Wren's expression. And I saw every different type: physical, emotional, and the kind that was soul-deep. "Do you want to tell us about it? Sometimes, that takes the power away."

Wren shuddered and gripped her legs tighter as if to shield her from the memories. She didn't answer immediately, just stared into the nothingness in front of her. "It was Bastian. He had me again."

Puck cursed and wrapped an arm around her. "He doesn't have you, and he's never getting his filthy paws on you again."

I wrapped my hand around one of Wren's calves, massaging it. The muscle might as well have been carved out of stone given how tense it was. "It's because you had a run-in with him. It's completely normal for your brain to try to process your fear when you sleep. It's actually quite healthy—"

"Locke," Puck said, cutting me off. "I don't think explaining the psychology to her will help."

I flushed.

Wren shook her head, dark strands of hair fluttering around

her. "No. It does, actually. Takes away some of the power." Her eyes welled with tears. "But at the end of the dream, he said you weren't coming for me. Said if you did, he'd rip out your hearts."

It was my turn to curse and push closer to Wren. "We will always come for you."

Wren started shaking her head again, more fervently this time. "You can't. I won't be the reason you die."

"Hey," Puck clipped, fury lacing the word. "No one is dying. And Bastian isn't getting any of us."

"You don't know that," Wren whispered. "He never gives up."

"Which is why we're going to take him out," Puck snarled.

Wren's eyes went wide. "You're what?"

"We're going to end him," Puck bit out. "We're working on a plan. But he won't scare us into reacting rashly. We'll be smart about it and get him when he least expects it."

Wren's whole body started to tremble. "You can't. He'll—"

Puck stole the words from her lips with a kiss, his mouth taking hers. She leaned into it, accepting his reassurance. When they broke apart, Wren sucked in a breath and leaned into me. My arms instantly went around her. I needed to remind myself that she was safe and here with us, where no one could hurt her.

"Trust us," Puck said.

It was part order and part question. Still, Wren nodded. "Okay."

My hands moved up and down her arms reassuringly. Telling her she wasn't alone.

"It feels like he'll always have control of me," she whispered. "Like those memories will haunt me forever."

My wolf snarled, hating that Wren had to live with the nightmares and had endured what caused them. I pulled her tighter against me. "They won't own you forever. You just have to replace them with good memories. The more of those you store up, the less the nightmares can get a foothold. They won't disappear forever, but they'll surface less and less often."

Wren looked my way, searching my eyes. "That's what happened for you?"

I nodded. I'd had more than my fair share of nightmares after living on the streets for years. But they'd lessened after King brought me into his pack, and I found my *true* family. And since Wren had come into my life, I hadn't had any.

"I love you." Wren spoke the words in a barely audible voice, but they still sounded like they'd been shot out of a cannon.

My entire body tensed as a low growl left my throat. "Say it again."

"I love you." The words were louder this time as Wren's gaze moved from me to Puck. "I love you both. You gave me a sense of belonging. Safety. You made me feel seen. I'll never be able to tell you how much that means to me."

"Show us," Puck growled. "Let us claim you. Claim us right back."

My dick hardened at Puck's words and what they would mean for the three of us: a bond that meant forever.

Wren looked from Puck to me and back again. "Yes."

CHAPTER THIRTY-FIVE

Wren

THE ENTIRE ROOM WENT SILENT FOR A SINGLE BREATH, and then Puck was on me, pushing me back against Locke. Claws lengthened from his fingertips, and a second later, he was shredding the T-shirt I'd borrowed from Brix.

"Hey," I protested. "I liked that shirt. It was the perfect level of softness."

A mischievous grin spread across his face. "Don't worry. Brix will get you another one. But now, I can do this."

Puck leaned forward and palmed my bare breast, sucking a nipple into his mouth. My back arched, and I let out a moan. It barely hit the air before Locke swallowed it whole.

There was something about Locke taking that sound, something Puck had coaxed from me, that had wetness gathering between my thighs. Locke's tongue stroked mine as Puck's swirled around my hard peak. He sucked hard again, sending a blaze of sensation from my nipple to my clit.

I arched into him further, pressing my breast firmly against his mouth in search of more. Puck tore his mouth from me, his eyes blazing. He cupped me between my thighs, my underwear already damp with need.

"Fucking scorching. Going to burn us both alive, aren't you?" Puck snarled.

My only answer came in the soft pants that left me as I pulled back from Locke's lips.

He reached around and palmed my breast, his hard length pressed against my ass cheeks.

I couldn't stop another soft moan from leaving me. Because I wanted them both. Wanted them to fill me, claim me, make me theirs.

"Please," I whispered.

"What do you think, Locke? Should we give our girl what she wants?"

Locke's fingers rolled my nipple. "She does beg so beautifully."

I pressed my ass harder against him as Puck rubbed me through the thin cotton of my boy shorts. He slid a finger under the cotton and cursed. "She's fucking soaked."

Locke let out a growl that had my core tightening around nothing, desperate to be filled. Puck fisted my underwear and pulled them free of my body so I was completely bare to them. He didn't wait. He dove between my thighs, lapping at me, his tongue exploring all of me as Locke palmed both breasts.

"Look how he eats you," Locke whispered in my ear. "How he's starving for everything your pussy will give him."

I whimpered, writhing against them both.

Puck slid two fingers inside me, curling them both as he sucked my clit, teasing the hood back.

"Don't come," Locke ordered. "Puck isn't done with his meal."

I let out a strangled sound. "I can't. I-it's too much."

"You can." The slightest alpha air slid into Locke's voice.

Puck's fingers drove in and out as his tongue flicked over that bundle of nerves.

"Please." Desperation curled around the word.

Then Puck's fingers and tongue were gone, and he was pulling me up to my knees. He tugged down his sweats, his cock springing free. He stroked it up and down, making saliva pool in my mouth.

"Tell us what you want," he gritted out.

"You," I whispered. "Both of you. Filling me. Taking me."

Puck looked behind me. "You heard her, brother. And we always give our mate what she wants."

Locke's fingers slid between my thighs, taking that wetness and dragging it back to my tight hole. His teeth nipped my neck. "I can't wait to feel all of you. Feel you taking all of me."

My pants came quicker as Puck's tip bumped my entrance and Locke's teased my rear. Puck slid in, letting out a groan of tortured pleasure.

"Better than I ever fucking dreamed, Birdie. I could die a happy man in this cunt. Feel me. All of me."

Each thrust moved him deeper as I gripped Puck's shoulders. My inner walls fluttered as Locke pressed in at my backside. I cried out as he thrust deeper. It was almost to the point of pain, teetering on that edge.

"Breathe deeply and push back against me," Locke growled.

I did as he ordered, and then he was fully inside me. Both of them. Moving with such perfect synchronicity that I writhed between them. It was nearly too much sensation, and I was lost to all of it. Every nerve ending in my body stood at attention.

Puck's canines lengthened, and I felt Locke's at my neck. At the exact same moment, they bit down. Puck on my shoulder, Locke on my neck. Pleasure like I'd never known shot through me. Pulsing in brutal waves that had light dancing across my vision.

As Locke retracted his teeth, I slammed mine down on Puck's shoulder. He howled as he came, his cum sparking my orgasm. I rode out wave after wave as he slammed into me, Locke meeting every thrust.

I pulled my teeth from his flesh, as he did the same to me, and reached for Locke. I sank my canines into his neck just below his jaw, and he came unhinged, thrusting into me with a manic ferocity that had me coming again as I took all my mates had to give.

As the last of the orgasm hit me, I succumbed, the darkness taking me under. But I wasn't scared to be in this dark; it promised that my mates would always keep me safe.

CHAPTER THIRTY-SIX

Wren

HEAT ENVELOPED ME LIKE THE COZIEST, COMFIEST DEN in the entire world, and I never wanted to leave. The sound of a throat clearing invaded my peacefulness, but I just burrowed deeper. This time, a raspy chuckle sounded, and I screwed up my face in annoyance.

"She's grumpy when someone wakes her after a sexfest. Even if it is almost eleven."

Hearing Brix's voice had the words finally computing and me jerking upright as Locke groaned and Puck told Brix to bugger off.

"Wha—?" I looked around the room, coming to a stop on Brix, who sat at the end of the bed.

He laughed full-out this time, motioning to his head. "Your hair is a little…"

I patted the top of my head, feeling a world of tangles and frizz. Apparently, the shower I barely remembered taking last night had left my hair in a state.

"Don't listen to him, Birdie. You look adorable." Puck kissed my shoulder and then sank back against the pillows.

Locke blinked a few times and reached for his glasses on the nightstand. "What time is it?"

"Almost eleven," Brix answered, putting a tray on the bed. "I brought breakfast."

My stomach rumbled louder than it ever had in my life.

Brix laughed again. "All that bonding works up an appetite. But I like the new marks."

My hand went to my neck and shoulder. I hadn't even seen what my new bonds looked like last night because I'd been too out of it.

"Here," Brix offered and pulled out his phone. He turned the camera app to selfie mode so I could use it as a mirror.

My fingers skimmed over the mark on my neck first. It was beautiful and so perfect. A lock with a heart in the middle of it. My nose stung as I found the answering mark on Locke's neck.

Then my hand moved to my shoulder and the mark there. It took me a second to place the meaning of an artistic house of sorts with a heart inside, but then I realized it was because Puck had given me shelter before he'd even met me, a safe place to stay when I'd needed it most.

A burn lit in my throat. "They're perfect," I croaked.

Brix leaned over the tray. "Just like you."

"Kiss-ass," Puck muttered.

Brix pulled back and scowled at him. "Hey, if you're not nice, you don't get French toast."

"I'm nice. I want French toast," I said quickly.

Brix chuckled and handed me a plate. He watched as I ate, the other guys digging in, too. Brix's fingers skimmed over my knee. "You have shadows in your eyes."

I swallowed hard, drowning my French toast with a sip of milk. "I had a bad dream last night."

"Bastian?" Brix growled.

I nodded, ducking my head. "Puck and Locke helped, but I think I need to control my fear a little more."

Brix's head cocked to the side in that animalistic way of his. "How so?"

"I think I'll feel better—stronger—if I can pour all that fear into training. You guys all have your individual strengths. I want you to teach them to me."

The room was quiet for a moment, and then Brix stood. He lifted me into the air and tossed me over his shoulder.

"Brix," I squealed. "What are you doing?"

He smacked my ass. "You said you wanted to train. Well, you're already late."

I rolled to the balls of my feet, my hands bracketing my head in a protective stance. Sweat rolled down my back and made my hair cling to my face. My muscles ached already.

I'd started my day with a ten-mile run with Brix, but his runs were a mix of sprints and parkour along with the distance. My body wasn't used to it. But that was good. It meant I was being challenged in new ways.

Then Puck had taken me through a jump rope routine that nearly had my heart beating out of my chest. And that was all before I'd started sparring lessons with Kingston.

My breaths came quickly, short pants that made my lungs burn. King sent out a testing jab that I blocked easily, but he didn't stop there. He dropped his shoulder for an uppercut that landed right in my ribs.

I winced, a flicker of pain blooming.

"Watch it," Puck snarled.

"I need the hits if I'm going to get better," I called before Kingston could answer.

King's pale-blue eyes darkened, a muscle in his cheek popping as I straightened and rolled to the balls of my feet again. I tried for a snap kick, but King easily dodged it. I let out a growl of frustration as I steadied myself again.

"Never wear your emotions on your sleeve," King instructed. "Because someone can take advantage."

He moved like it was effortless, a work of performance art. He struck out with a leg sweep, taking mine out from under me. I was already falling, but he caught me behind the neck, gentling my landing.

The air still whooshed from my lungs as King straddled me, searching my face. "We're done," he said, a finality ringing in his words.

"But—"

"No buts," he clipped, pushing to his feet and offering me a hand. "We'll do more tomorrow, but training when you're exhausted will only get you injured."

I knew he had a point, but I still huffed out a breath of annoyance as I righted myself.

"Don't pout," Puck said, amusement lacing his tone. "Locke went to get lunch and your next lesson."

That piqued my interest.

"Just call me your errand boy," Locke called as he entered the gym, his arms laden with too many bags to count.

Ender pushed off the far wall, the place he'd stayed throughout my training with Puck and King, simply watching with that astute stare of his. "I got it."

"You're the one who should be helping," Locke shot at Puck. "How many sandwiches did you make?"

Puck just grinned and took another bag from Locke. "I knew we'd work up an appetite."

We all settled on the floor, devouring the gourmet creations Puck had dreamed up. Turkey sandwiches with sharp cheddar and cranberry sauce. Egg salad with bacon and heirloom tomatoes. Steak sandwiches with caramelized onions and garlic aioli.

"Okay," Locke said around a mouthful of food. "I take it back. We needed all the options."

Puck chuckled. "You're welcome."

I swallowed my last bite, chasing it with a sip of Coke, and then flopped back onto the mat. "Whatever's next, you're going to have to carry me. I've descended into a food coma."

"You don't have to move a single step," Locke said, reaching for another bag.

I glanced over at him. "You're up?"

He nodded.

"More lock picking?" I pushed back to sitting, eager to see what he had for me.

"Not exactly." Locke pulled out what looked like zip ties.

A chill skated down my spine. How many times had Bastian and his men used bindings like that to keep me in place?

Kingston leaned over and laid his hand over mine. "If it's too much, just say the word."

I shook my head. "No. This is good." It was exactly the sort of thing I needed to learn to take my power back.

Locke pushed to his feet and offered me a hand. I took it, shaking off any lingering anxiety.

"I'm going to bind your hands in front first. These are shifter-resistant zip ties—the kind that are harder for us to break," he explained, showing me the plastic lengths.

"Let's do this," I said, squaring my shoulders and holding out my hands.

Locke quickly put the ties on so they bit into my skin but didn't cut off circulation. "Test them."

I tugged gently, then harder. As far as I could tell, there was no way I could get them off without losing a hand in the process.

"Good," Locke said. "See this?" He pointed at the bracket holding the plastic in place.

"Sure."

"That's what we need to focus on breaking, not the plastic cord itself."

Interesting. Whenever I'd been tied up in the past, I'd always tried to fray the length. I looked up at Locke. "How?"

"Pressure and force."

"Science nerd," Puck called.

"A science nerd who has saved your ass more than once," Locke shot back.

Puck just grinned and shot me a wink. "He's right."

I shook my head and turned back to Locke. "Show me."

He held his hands in front of him as if they were bound. "Lift your hands as far away from your body as you can."

I mirrored his movement with my arms, studying all the angles.

"Good. Now, what you'll do is bring your hands down in one swift movement, as fast as you can." Locke executed the action. "If there's enough force, the bracket will pop right off."

It made sense, but it would hurt like hell if it didn't work. I made the motion slowly at first, ensuring I had it down. Then, taking a deep breath, I did it at full speed.

My fists slammed into my stomach and the ties burned the hell out of my wrists, but no bracket broke. I coughed and doubled over.

Locke muttered a curse and moved in to help me straighten.

"You didn't commit." The voice was one I'd only heard a couple of times today. Now, it carried criticism as Ender glared at me.

"Gee, thanks," I muttered as I stood up fully.

"You would've had it if you hadn't let doubt get in your way at the last second. You can do this. Don't doubt yourself," he commanded.

A flicker of warmth took root somewhere deep. Because Ender's critique was how he showed he cared.

Squaring my shoulders, I lifted my hands again. This time, I closed my eyes. I remembered how powerless I'd felt at the hands of Bastian and his men, all the pain they'd caused me over the years. I let those memories fuel my anger. And as my wolf snarled within me, I slammed my hands against my body. Pain flared at my wrists, but it was fleeting because a pop sounded, and then I was free.

My eyes flew open, a grin stretching across my lips. "It worked."

Locke pulled me in for a quick hug. "Told you. Certified badass."

"Are there different techniques if your hands are behind you or tethered to stationary objects?"

Locke nodded. "We can work on a different one each day."

Excitement bubbled. "Thanks—"

Movement caught my eye, and I whirled, catching the bo staff just before it smacked me in the face.

"Come on, Kitten," Ender growled. "Let's go."

CHAPTER THIRTY-SEVEN

Ender

TODAY HAD BEEN PURE AND UTTER TORTURE—AND IN every way imaginable. Watching Wren push herself to the point of exhaustion. Watching her endure physical and emotional pain. But she never stopped. She was too damn strong for that.

But worse? I'd had to watch my brothers touching her. The way Brix's expression went soft as he leaned in to whisper encouragements in her ear. How King held her hand for just a beat longer than necessary when he pulled her to her feet. Puck's lingering kisses and the way his fingers tangled in her hair. How Locke wrapped her in his arms, giving her a place to rest.

I hated them all for it. And they were my *brothers*. My family of choice. But my wolf was so jealous he wanted to rip them limb from limb. And my human half wanted to join him.

My back teeth ground together as I gripped my bo staff.

Sparring was exactly what I needed, and maybe simply being in Wren's presence would help my wolf get himself in check.

"You trying to give me a black eye or a broken nose?" Wren clipped.

"You should always be aware of your surroundings. Expect the unexpected."

Wren let out a low growl as she stalked toward the fight ring. "If that's a pep talk, you might want to take some lessons from Princess."

Annoyance flitted through me. Even my damn cat was in love with Wren. The worst part? I didn't blame her or any of them.

My fingers tightened around the staff. "You don't need my coddling. You have four other mates for that."

A variety of growls lit the air, and I knew King would likely kick my ass later for the comment. But I'd welcome it, anything to distract me from the clawing need pulling me down to hell.

"I'll show you coddling," Wren muttered.

She struck out with her staff, connecting with mine in a surprising show of force. My lips twitched. My kitten was feisty.

We circled each other, striking with testing jabs. Gods, she was a vision. One I could watch for eternity and never get tired. Wren was so damn petite, but every inch of her packed a punch that showed just how strong she was.

Her staff hit mine with a force that had me stumbling back a step.

"You're losing your touch, End," Puck called. I didn't miss Brix's snicker of agreement. *Assholes.*

I focused, increasing my speed. The moment my bo hit Wren's, I was already moving to the next strike. She cursed, fighting to keep up with me. Her chest heaved in her tempting workout tank, the swells beneath it rising and falling with each pant.

"You can't let your fatigue get the best of you," I gritted out as one of my hits nearly took Wren down.

She bared her teeth at me. "Next time, you have to do all the other training with me. *Then* we'll spar."

"She has a point," Locke yelled. "It's not exactly fair."

My lip curled as I executed a spin move and took Wren by surprise. "Life isn't fair. You and your opponent will never go through the exact same things on the exact same day."

Wren grunted as my staff clipped her ribs. "What are you, some life coach guru?"

Puck snickered, and I sent him a glare. It was just a split second of distraction, but Wren didn't let it go to waste. Her staff struck my lower back, and I let out a pained grunt. But she showed no mercy. Instead, she pressed on the back of my knee until I started to go down.

But I wasn't about to let the little kitten win. I dipped into a forward roll, then sprang up and spun around.

"What the hell?" Wren muttered.

I was already on her, my staff about to come down hard on her shoulder. She spun and lifted her bo to block at the last second.

"Good," I praised. "Maybe there's hope for you yet."

She scowled at me, my patronizing words only stoking her anger and fueling her fire for battle.

"Use it," I growled. "Whatever your opponent throws at you, let it fuel you for the fight to come."

"Well, I'd say you give me plenty of fuel with your assholery," Wren shot back as she swung her bo in an arc of beauty. The move wasn't textbook, but that was part of what made it work. It was surprising, just like her.

The blow hit me in the shoulder, the pain stunning me for a moment. Wren didn't wait. The staff swung around and swept my legs out from under me. My back hit the mat with a force that shoved all the air from my lungs, and then Wren had the end of her bo pointed right at my throat.

"Yield," she growled.

My eyes flared, and my dick hardened. *Fuck.* She was stunning.

"You forgot one thing," I rasped.

Wren arched a brow. "And that is?"

"It's not over till it's over." I grabbed her staff and yanked it hard, throwing her off-balance. I pulled Wren to the mat and then rolled on top of her, pressing a forearm to her throat. We were close—so close the scent of wildflowers and rain was all around me. So strong I swore I could taste it on my tongue.

"Yield," I whispered against her lips.

Wren's turquoise eyes flashed silver. "Never."

"That could get you dead in the wrong circumstances." But damn if I didn't admire the hell out of it.

"So be it." She met my gaze, nothing but defiance in her stare.

Gods, I wanted to kiss her. To know what her skin tasted like. To bury myself so deep inside her it would brand her for all eternity.

Fucking hell.

I was off Wren faster than she could blink, jumping to my feet and stalking toward the gym door. I needed a cold shower.

CHAPTER THIRTY-EIGHT

Wren

EVERYTHING HURT. I'D WOKEN WITH ACHING MUSCLES AND a heaviness in my bones I couldn't shake. But that hadn't stopped Brix from forcing me into a morning parkour run session or King from making me spar for an hour.

Okay, the *forcing* wasn't exactly true, but I did complain the whole time. The fact that I'd had to be on my feet at Arcane for hours afterward hadn't helped.

Large hands landed on my shoulders, and fingers began kneading the muscles there. I moaned, my lids falling closed as Puck's smoky whiskey scent swirled around me. "Please, never stop. I'll give you my soul if you do this forever."

Puck let out a husky chuckle. "I don't mind the idea of owning you."

"You would, you overbearing alpha," I muttered.

He pressed a kiss to my hair. "We've only got another hour before closing. Then you can go straight to bed."

Gods, that sounded like heaven. Fluffy pillows. Warm bodies. And sleep that lasted for at least twelve hours.

"Do you want me to make you a snack? We're pretty slow—"

As if he'd tempted fate, the front door opened, cutting off Puck's words. I forced myself to lift my lids and immediately wanted to close my eyes again. Because if I closed them, I could ignore that Cressida and her two bitchy minions, Dara and Siena, had just walked in.

Puck let out a low, rumbling growl. "What did I say about you coming here?"

Cressida sent him a simpering, contrite look that was obviously fake. "We're here to apologize. You were right. I was jealous. I thought we shared something special, and I wasn't ready to see you move on. But Wren didn't deserve me being mean." Her gaze flicked to me ever so briefly. "I'm sorry."

She spoke both my name and *sorry* as if she'd tasted something bad, then turned her glare on her friends. They both quickly mumbled apologies, as well.

Puck pulled me into him and brushed the hair back from my face. "What do you think?"

The last thing I wanted was to have these three bitches harboring hatred because I got them kicked out of the only bar in town. "It's fine. They can stay."

Puck's gaze didn't move from my face for a moment, as if he was making sure I was certain. Then he glanced at them. "You pull one move that's even a little suspect, and you're out. And next time, it'll be for life."

Siena paled at that, but I could see the annoyance in Cressida's gaze. I had a feeling Cress would be out on her ass before long.

"What'll you have?" Puck asked.

The ladies ordered cocktails, and Puck got to work filling their orders. I took that as my excuse to visit the few tables with patrons. A couple of mechanics from the local shop were finishing up their round of beers, a tourist couple with hearts in their eyes and hands in places that said they were getting lucky later lingered but asked for the bill, and a woman who looked vaguely familiar had settled in with a book and a glass of wine.

I got the check for the mechanics and the couple, but when I stopped at the woman's table, she startled then flushed. "Sorry. Head in the clouds," she muttered.

"It's no problem," I said with a smile. "Do you want another glass before we close? It's about to be last call."

She glanced up at the clock on the wall. "Oh, goodness. I really have lost track of time."

"Must be a good book."

"The best," she said, her lips twitching. "But I'd better get going. Thanks for the wine."

"Anytime," I said, heading back to the bar to get my rag and cleaning spray.

Cressida's high-pitched laugh grated on my nerves, but I shoved the annoyance down as I reached for my supplies.

"Need any help?" Puck asked hopefully.

"Sorry, buddy. You're stuck behind the bar."

His green eyes sparked with gold. "Birdie...you know what that does to me."

I grinned. "Too bad you can't do anything about it."

"Oh, I can't?" Puck moved in a flash, grabbing me around the waist and taking my mouth. My lips parted, and his tongue stroked in. I couldn't hold back the moan as his taste teased my tongue.

One of the mechanics hooted while someone else started clapping. Puck righted me, and I stared at him, blinking and trying to steady myself.

"What was that you were saying, Birdie?" Puck asked innocently.

I scowled at him. "I'm gonna get you back for that."

"Sure, you will," he said, laughter in his voice.

"You tell him, Wren," one of the mechanics called as he headed out the door, his buddies in tow.

The woman from the tourist couple gave me a thumbs-up as she took her boyfriend's hand, and I couldn't help but giggle. The sound died on my lips as I met Cressida's furious glare. It was almost comical how angry she was. So, I just smiled at her. "Something to say?"

She downed the rest of her drink in one swig and slid off her stool. "I think the ambience in here leaves a little something to be desired."

"Aw, shucks. We'll miss you," I singsonged.

Puck choked on a laugh as Cressida's henchmen followed her out. "Cleared 'em out with fifteen minutes to spare. I'm in awe of you, Birdie."

"As you should be."

We made quick work of cleaning up. I handled the tables while Puck followed behind me with the broom. Before long, we were ready to go.

Stepping out into the night, I breathed deeply. The pine air swirled around me, clearing away the scents of the day. Having shifter senses in a confined space for so many hours could be a lot, and as tired as I was, my wolf craved a run.

I started toward Puck's SUV, parked a few spots down, but stilled as I scented something that didn't belong.

Fox.

And I wasn't talking about the wild animal. I meant shifter. I opened my mouth to yell, but it was too late. A blade was already headed straight for me.

CHAPTER THIRTY-NINE

Puck

LOCKING THE DEADBOLT, I PULLED OUT MY KEY AND shoved it into my pocket. As I turned to head for the SUV, I froze. Panic speared through me as a man with red hair and a scraggly beard lunged for Wren, a knife glinting in the building's lights.

I shouted and jerked into action, running for Wren, but it was too late.

She struck out with a roundhouse kick, sending the blade clattering to the pavement.

The man cursed and lifted his hands, shifting into a fighting stance, a sneer on his face. "You think you can take me, submissive? I can smell your weakness on you."

It was probably the dumbest thing someone could say to Wren, but she didn't let her rage show; she used it like Ender had instructed, letting it fuel a jab to his jaw.

The man's head snapped back with a vicious crack, making

curse again. He was quicker this time, striking out with a hook. But Wren was too fast for him. She ducked the punch and answered with one to his ribs. "What do you want?" she growled.

The redhead's lip curled. "There's a price on your head, and I'm here to collect."

Hell. The last thing we needed was the dark corners of the supernatural community trying to collect Wren for a reward.

She didn't really appreciate it either because she hit him with a blow to the face that ended in a sickening crunch.

The man doubled over, cupping his face. "You broke my fucking nose."

"You're lucky that's all I broke," she snarled, sweeping in behind him and holding him in a choke hold.

The guy clawed at her arm, trying to get free, but it was useless. In a matter of seconds, he went limp. She dropped him to the pavement, barely even breathing harder than when it all started.

I looked from her to him and back again. "I guess you really didn't need me, after all, Birdie."

She grinned at me. "I could use your help getting him into the back."

I chuckled, beeping my key fob to open the hatch. "I'm at your service."

Wren grabbed the man's feet while I lifted him from his armpits, my nose wrinkling at his stench. I could scent the drugs running through his system. No wonder he was out for money. He needed to score another hit.

"Let's go," Wren muttered, shoving him in. "He'll only be out for thirty minutes or so."

I slammed the back hatch. "I'm rolling down all the windows so I don't upchuck."

Wren chuckled and patted me on the shoulder. "Don't worry, buddy. We can get you some ginger ale for that sensitive stomach when we get home."

I flipped her off. "You get locked in a car with his stinky ass, and you'd be vomming, too."

She grinned as she hopped in, but her nose wrinkled almost immediately. "Okay, you're right."

"Told you." I started up the SUV and rolled down all the windows. As I backed out of the parking spot, I hit the phone icon on the wheel. "Call Kingston."

The phone rang through the speakers. A second later, King's voice filled the SUV. "Everything okay?"

"Just fine and dandy, but can you have everyone meet us in front of the house in ten? We've got something to show you."

"What?" King growled.

"It's a surprise," I said, grinning at Wren. She just shook her head and rolled her eyes.

"What. Kind. Of. Surprise?"

"One you have to wait for." I hit End on the call before King could go all alpha on me.

Wren turned to face me. "You know he's gonna kick your ass for that."

I shrugged. "Worth it."

I made the drive as quickly as possible without risking getting pulled over because it wasn't like I'd be able to explain the dude in the back.

As we approached the gate, Wren reached over and clicked the remote. The gates swung open, and we sailed through. By the time we got to the house, the rest of the guys were ready and waiting, a mixture of expressions on their faces. Pissed the hell off. Annoyed. Curious. And some mix of the three.

I slowed to a stop, and Wren slid out of the passenger seat. As I climbed out, I saw King stalking toward her, his gaze sliding over her face. "You're okay?"

"I'm great," she said with a smile. "We've got a little something for you in the SUV, though."

"What?" King asked warily.

"The fox shifter who tried to grab Wren," I answered helpfully.

Brix's expression went as cold as ice, pure silver bleeding into his eyes. "You mean the fox shifter who's about to have his skin peeled from his body?"

"Oh, goody," I cheered. "The psycho twins at work again."

"Show us the shifter," King growled.

Locke moved into Wren's space. "You sure you're okay?"

She nodded and gave him a quick kiss. "Just peachy."

"Birdie kicked his ass," I informed them.

"Good," Brix growled, prowling toward the back of the SUV as the hatch opened.

Ender was right there with him, his amber eyes now a brown so dark they were almost black. He surveyed the pathetic shifter in the trunk. "Who's ready to remove some organs?"

CHAPTER FORTY

Ender

"I'M GOING WITH YOU." THE FINALITY IN WREN'S TONE WAS as admirable as her glare. But as she crossed her arms, the only thing she managed to do was thrust her breasts upward, which made half of us let out a variety of groans.

"Seriously?" she clipped.

Puck's lips twitched. "Doesn't matter if we're in the middle of a war. You show us a hint of what you're hiding under that tank, and we'll always be appreciative."

Wren rolled her eyes. "Men."

But the fact that she was wearing a tank to begin with had some foreign sensation shifting through my chest. When we first met her, she had covered her scars, not wanting the world to see them. But as time passed, she'd begun to care less and less what others saw or thought.

I fucking loved that.

What I didn't love was the idea of her going with us to…

question the fox shifter. The last thing she needed was to see that bloodshed.

"I'm going with you," she said again as if reading my thoughts.

"Wren," Kingston began.

"I can handle it," she gritted out.

"Of course, you can," he said quickly, truth ringing in his tone.

She blinked a few times. "Okay. Then—"

"It's us who can't handle it," King explained. "Especially those who've bonded with you recently. You know that puts them on edge. Once the fox is awake, their wolves won't be able to handle having you near the shifter who tried to harm you."

Bonded.

Just hearing King say the word made jealousy surge to the surface and had my wolf snapping at me. He hated that we hadn't claimed Wren. And rightfully blamed me for it.

That stew of reactions only stoked my annoyance and anger—emotions I'd be sure to take out on our fox shifter friend.

Wren stared at Kingston for a long moment, then her shoulders slumped in defeat. "Fine. I'll stay here."

Locke moved into her space and wrapped his arm around her. "I'll stay with you."

Wren burrowed into his side. "You don't have to."

"You know I'm not one for the whole violence thing," he said, guiding her toward the house.

My lip curled, and the urge to rip his arm from around Wren was strong.

"Watch your wolf," Brix said, his voice low.

My gaze snapped to him. "What? You're going to lecture me now that you have a fucking girlfriend?"

Brix didn't show any signs of reaction, which only annoyed me more. "You've been shoving his instincts down," he went on. "That's never a good cocktail."

"Mind your own damn business." I stalked to the back of the

SUV and slammed the hatch. "Are we going to do this, or are we going to stand around all night with our thumbs up our asses?"

"He's in a delightful mood," Puck muttered, climbing into the driver's seat.

I ripped open the door to the back seat, and it was a miracle I didn't take the thing off its hinges. Sliding in, I slammed the door behind me and immediately wanted to rip the vehicle apart. The stench of fox and drugs was pungent, even with the windows open. I let out a snarl.

"Do I have to sit next to him?" Brix muttered from outside.

"You could always take the back with the fox," King suggested as he climbed into the passenger seat.

"Might be better," Brix groused as he sat next to me and Puck started the engine.

"Cry me a fucking river," I snapped.

Puck guided the SUV down the gravel road that led deeper into our territory. "I think he might be hangry."

"It's horny you're thinking of," King offered.

"Like you're not? You've been living in a perpetual state of blue balls," I shot back.

He shrugged, watching the road as he always did when his alert system was heightened. "I've made peace with it. You're just being a cranky ass."

I turned, scowling out the window and hoping the fresh breeze would clear away the awful scents in the vehicle.

The rest of the guys remained quiet, probably not wanting to stoke my wrath. Smart.

It took us about ten minutes to get to the spot we'd designated as a jail and detention center of sorts. We didn't need to use it often because our territory was fairly well hidden, but if someone trespassed or tried to do us harm, this was where they ended up so they could be questioned and...dealt with.

Puck slowed to a stop in front of what looked like a standard cabin. But when you got inside, there were two cells and an area where prisoners could be questioned. It looked pretty damn terrifying. But then again, there was a reason we had the reputations we did.

We slid out of the SUV, Puck pushing the button for the back hatch.

"I'll get the fox. If you let End take him in there, he'll be dead before we reach the threshold," Brix said, moving to the back.

Puck shook his head. "When did you become the reasonable one?"

"Probably since Wren put his balls on a chain," I muttered.

A smack landed on the back of my head, courtesy of King. "Watch it."

My back teeth ground together, but I bit my tongue and followed Puck into the cabin. He flicked on the lights, illuminating the space and the dust-covered surfaces. I moved around, opening windows, not wanting to be closed in with the scent of drugs once they brought the fox in.

A soft groan sounded as Brix carried the man inside. He tossed the shifter into a metal chair and fastened his wrists and ankles to the arms and legs with shifter-proof chains. The fox wouldn't be going anywhere.

Puck strode over with a syringe he'd gotten from the supply closet. Sliding the needle into the man's arm, he hit the plunger. The serum would keep the man from shifting into his fox form.

Once all the windows were open, I stalked back to the fox and waited. The four of us formed a half circle around the shifter, Kingston taking center. It took a few minutes for the man to come around, but the second he did, he writhed against the bindings. I watched as he tried to bring on the change and call on his other half, but he couldn't.

"What the hell did you give me?" he snarled, spittle flying.

"Just a little something to keep the fox at bay," Puck singsonged. "Don't pretend like you give a damn what poison you put in your veins."

The man sniffed. "I don't know what you're talking about."

Kingston let out a low growl that carried the dominance of a true alpha. The man snapped his mouth closed, sweat breaking out on his brow. King crossed his arms over his chest and stepped forward. "Do you know who we are?"

Defiance lit in the fox's eyes, and I knew he was about to make a dumb play. "Probably the pack of that bitch."

A muscle popped in King's cheek. "Did you take the time to find out what pack the woman you sought to kidnap was a part of?"

"Don't fuckin' matter," the man spat.

"But it does," King cooed. "Maybe you've heard of us. The Diablos ring a bell?"

The blood didn't drain from the fox's face. It disappeared altogether, and the man's eyes went so wide you could see more whites than irises. "I-I-I didn't know. They didn't say. I-I wouldn't have."

"Want to know what else?" King said, baring his teeth. "She's. Our. Mate."

My wolf howled at that, demanding justice and blood.

A wet spot bloomed on the man's jeans, darkening the denim.

"Aw, hell," Puck muttered. "Why do they always piss themselves?"

"It's better than the vomit," Brix muttered.

"That always comes later," Puck argued. "When we start removing fingers and toes."

"I'll tell you whatever you want. I swear. I just—" The fox closed his eyes. "Just make my death swift. Promise."

I scoffed. The man had no honor. No strength. And my wolf wouldn't even get the joy of breaking him.

"Tell us who hired you," King ordered.

"No one," the man said.

King snarled.

"I swear! There's a reward on the open market. For anyone who can grab the girl with the scarred face in Crescent Creek."

The series of growls that lit the air had the fox trembling.

"Who?" King snapped.

"Red River."

This time, the growls were deafening. My wolf raked at my insides, demanding freedom. He wanted nothing more than the taste of Bastian Boudreaux's blood on his tongue.

"Tell. Me. Everything," Kingston gritted out.

"It, uh, went out on the black market. A call for people to bring her to Red River alive. I guess Boudreaux wants to make an example of her," the fox said, his gaze jumping around the room.

"How so?" Brix snarled, fur rippling over his arms.

"H-he wants to breed her then kill her."

Brix let out a howl that was pain and rage all wrapped into one.

Kingston's expression had gone completely cold, his face nearly unrecognizable. "The price. Tell me the price."

"Ten million for her alive," the fox whispered.

I couldn't wait any longer. I knew no additional information would be useful, so I stalked forward, bent down, and got in the bastard's face.

"Wren. Her name is Wren."

"O-okay."

"Say her name," I snarled.

"Wren," he whispered.

"Remember it and take it to hell with you."

My claws lengthened, and I punched my fist into his chest, fingers clamping around his heart, feeling it beat against my palm. Then I tore it straight out of his rib cage, relishing the feel of his blood coating my arm.

But it wasn't enough. Not even close. It wouldn't be until I'd wiped every enemy of Wren's from the planet.

CHAPTER FORTY-ONE

Wren

LOCKE PULLED ME ONTO HIS LAP AND NUZZLED MY NECK. This was always his way of showing comfort—giving me the physical contact I'd lacked for so many years. But not even Locke's cuddles could distract me from what I knew was happening.

I wasn't ignorant of how the shifter world worked. As beautiful as it was, it could be equally brutal at times. And if you moved against someone's mate, you paid the price. But there was information to be gathered first.

Locke's fingers slid under the hem of my T-shirt and traced a lopsided figure eight on my back. "Want to watch a movie?"

"That's okay." I didn't think I could focus on anything right now.

"We could play a video game," he offered.

"No thanks."

"We could make out."

That had a surprised laugh bubbling out of me. I pulled back to take him in. "I do like making out with you."

A hint of pink hit Locke's cheeks. "Good to know."

I brushed the brown strands from his face, taking in the beautiful gray eyes behind his black-framed glasses. "I love you."

Sparks of silver danced in those eyes. "I love you, too. More than you'll ever know."

"I feel it," I whispered. "Every single day."

And it was true. It was like this foreign energy swirling around me at every moment. A reassuring breeze and phantom presence that was always with me.

"I'm glad," Locke rasped. His hold on me tightened a fraction. "I hate that he could've hurt you tonight—or worse."

"Hey," I said, burrowing deeper into him. "I'm fine. Better than. I kicked his ass. So, I'm feeling pretty damn badass at the moment."

One corner of Locke's mouth kicked up. "As you should."

I laid a hand over his heart, feeling the beat of it beneath my palm. "I'm sorry I scared you."

Locke stared up into my face. "Having someone so vital to me walking around out there, exposed, is new for me."

"I get that. It's…unnerving." I felt like that when I left the guys. And even on the days when Puck worked the bar with me, I still felt so…vulnerable.

"I was going to go with terrifying, but…"

I chuckled. "Okay, maybe that's more honest."

Locke brushed a strand of hair out of my face and tucked it behind my ear. "We'll get used to it. And I think all of us will rest a little easier once we've dealt with Red River."

My stomach cramped because it wasn't just Red River. It was the Death Walkers and, even though we hadn't heard a peep from them recently, the dark mages. Threats would always be circling. We just had to learn to live with it.

"I don't want to hide away forever," I whispered.

Locke's brows pulled together. "What do you mean?"

"There's always going to be danger out there. But I don't want it to make us stop living. If we do…then what are we fighting for?"

Locke brought my head down to his, our foreheads touching. "You're wise, you know that?"

"If the genius thinks I'm wise, I'm calling that an honorary college degree."

Locke pulled back, studying me. "Did you want to go to college?"

I worried a spot on the inside of my cheek. "I did a couple of terms at Evergreen University. I wanted to finish and get a degree, but…"

"You had to run?" he asked.

I nodded. "When my friend Hayden got caught up in a dragon shifter war, it got too hot in Ember Hollow. Supernaturals of all kinds flooded the town, and I knew it was only a matter of time before someone put two and two together and informed Bastian of where I was."

Locke threaded his fingers through mine. "I'm sorry, Wren."

"It's not your fault."

"I know, but I still wish you could've finished your degree." He stilled for a moment. "Would you want to? Finish it, I mean."

I hadn't thought about it in so long. When I was forced to leave Evergreen, I'd lost the scholarship that went with it—the only way to complete my studies. But now that I was living with the guys, I could save all the money I made at Arcane. I could afford classes if I really wanted to.

"I think I would like to," I admitted.

Locke grinned and lifted me off his lap, setting me beside him. He reached for his laptop on the coffee table and flipped it open. "There are a ton of different colleges and universities not that far from here. What were you majoring in?"

I worried the corner of my lip. "I hadn't declared yet."

He turned to look at me. "If you could do *anything*, what would it be?"

I froze. When I started at Evergreen, my only thought had been to find a career that could make me decent money and keep me under the radar. Maybe accounting. But if those were no longer my guidelines, I could do anything.

Struggling to swallow, I cleared my throat. "I think I might like to get a degree in psychology."

Everything about Locke gentled in that moment. "My little empath," he whispered.

My lips twitched as I shrugged. "I guess it's built into me. I just—I think I could help people with trauma. Maybe I can help in ways beyond just my supernatural gift."

Locke leaned into me and brushed his lips against mine. "I love that idea. I'll research all the schools with psych programs and send you a list."

Warmth spread through me at his care. "Thank you. I'm so lucky to have you."

A shy grin spread across his face. He opened his mouth to say something but was cut off by the sound of the front door opening. I was on my feet in a flash, ready for the guys as they entered the living room.

My stomach dropped at the sight of them. Their expressions ran the gambit from stormy to fury-filled. And they looked like they were all freshly showered. No, not showered. I scented creek water on their skin. Which meant things had gotten bloody.

"What happened?" I croaked. "Where is he?"

Ender's eyes were almost black as his gaze slid to me. "Dead. And his heart is on its way to your father."

CHAPTER FORTY-TWO

Wren

I STARED AT THE MAN KNOWN BY MANY AS SIMPLY THE Archer, a man who made his way in the world as an assassin. It shouldn't have surprised me that Ender would have nothing but apathy about killing another living being. But the fact that he'd sent the man's heart to my father was plain stupid.

"You what?" I snapped.

Ender's jaw worked back and forth. "I wrapped up the drug-drenched organ and sent it by courier to the last place we know your father stayed. Two towns over."

Nausea slid through me. "You know where he is?"

King stepped forward and shook his head. "Not currently. But we were able to track certain movements. Bastian and some of his men stayed at a small hotel in Ridgewater. We're guessing that if a package is delivered to him there, they'll call him to pick it up."

"And you'll what? Pop out of the trees and take him out?" I asked incredulously.

"We know he won't be the one to get it," Puck assured me. "He's too chickenshit for that. He hides behind his enforcers and doesn't care if they die because of him."

At least they understood how Bastian operated. But it still begged the question... "Then, why? What's the point? Other than to piss him the hell off?"

"It sends a message," Brix ground out, still struggling to deal with his fury.

"Who cares about a damn message?" I snapped. The whole idea was reckless. It would only make my father angrier and more determined to take us all out.

"To throw him off his game," Puck said quietly. "He won't expect us to know where he was, and dispatching someone who answered his reward call this quickly will have him thinking twice, as well."

Acid churned in my stomach. "Reward call?" I knew there'd been a reward for my capture and return to Red River, but this sounded different.

The guys shared a look as Locke moved in behind me, lending me his strength. "Tell her," Locke said, his voice low. "She can handle it."

Kingston met my gaze, his eyes alarmingly vacant. "Your father put out a ten-million-dollar reward for your capture and return. He said he wants to breed you and then kill you publicly as a warning to those who think to cross him."

My mouth went dry. It shouldn't have been a shock. I already knew the breeding part, and I could've guessed the killing piece. But my mind got stuck on the ten million dollars.

Bastian was the greediest, most tight-fisted person I knew. He spent money on himself, buying more lavish homes and cars, and rewarded his inner circle to keep them loyal. But that was it. The past reward for my capture was a hundred grand.

Ten million dollars.

"I didn't know how much he hated me," I croaked. Ten million pieces of hatred. Ten million reasons for anyone to betray me.

Pressure built behind my eyes as a burn lit in my throat. It was too much. I hadn't asked him for anything. Not one thing. My mother hadn't either. We'd just wanted to live.

He'd stolen her life. Now, he wanted to take mine, too.

"Birdie." Puck strode across the room, pulling me into his arms. "He's not going to get you."

"No, he's fucking not," Brix snarled.

"I put out a different sort of call," King said, his voice carrying coldness. "I let it be known far and wide that you are under The Diablos' protection. That you are *mated* to The Diablos. And if anyone so much as tries to harm a hair on your head, they will be hunted into eternity."

I pulled out of Puck's hold but stayed close to him and Locke. My gaze was only for Kingston, though. Because I knew what this cost him. King didn't want to be known for his cruelty or brutality. The Diablos were a reputation and name bestowed on him and the others by evil men. But King was nothing but goodness.

Taking a deep breath, I crossed to him, standing so close our shoes almost touched. "Thank you," I whispered. Then I closed the tiny distance and let the scents of pine and mint swirl around me. I swept my lips across King's in the barest touch before stepping back and meeting his eyes. "Thank you."

Kingston let out a shuddering breath, color and life bleeding back into his face. "I'd do anything for you, Little Warrior. *Anything*."

I knew it, too. And it had warmth flooding back into me. Something else, as well. Hope.

My hands fisted as I fought back nerves. "Do you think… could we all stay together tonight?"

The room went silent around me, and I couldn't force my gaze to meet any of theirs. I was too anxious about the possible responses. A hand slid through mine, and I instantly recognized Puck's scent.

"Come on. We want to show you something," he said, tugging me up the stairs.

I'd ventured to the second level a handful of times. That was where Brix, Ender, and Locke had bedrooms. But Puck didn't stop on the second floor; he kept right on going.

"I thought the third floor was just attic space," I said.

"It was," Puck confirmed. "But we've been changing it into something else every moment you've been at work or the gym."

He pushed open a door and flipped on the lights. I couldn't help the gasp that fled my lips at the sight in front of me. The room was massive and absolutely stunning. A blend of modern and rustic, it carried elements of us all.

On a far wall was a painting of an archer done in an impressionist style but with colors that blended perfectly with the rest of the room—blues, grays, and the occasional pop of maroon to bring color. There was a dresser below the painting with an antique cocktail set on top that instantly made me think of Puck.

On the opposite side of the space, a corner had been turned into a library of sorts—shelves with books, a rustic leather couch, and overstuffed chairs. There were rusted, oversized locks used as bookends and an antique dagger representing Locke and Brix. And then there was the fighter art. An abstract recreation of the ring and two fighters within.

Pieces of each of my guys. My nose stung as I blinked back tears. "It's perfect."

"What about the bed?" Puck asked, waggling his eyebrows as King smacked him.

I choked on a laugh as I took in the bed that looked large enough to fit an entire football team. "That's perfect, too."

Locke moved in behind me, wrapped his arms around my chest, and pulled me back against him. "You really like it?"

"It's everything," I whispered. Because it was all of us becoming one. And I couldn't have asked for anything more.

CHAPTER FORTY-THREE

Wren

I WOKE TO A WHOLE NEW LEVEL OF WARMTH. WARMTH AND grumbling.

"Your hard-on is poking me in the ass," Puck snarled at Brix.

"Then you shouldn't have hogged Wren last night. Sacrifices must be made," Brix said, rolling onto his back.

"That's better than having King kneeing you in the spleen all night," Locke muttered.

I pushed myself up against the pillows and then burst out laughing. The five of us were taking up only about a third of the massive bed. "Why didn't you guys spread out?"

King pushed up onto one elbow and pressed a kiss to my bare shoulder. "Because we all wanted to be close to you."

The sentiment had my heart squeezing, but my gaze sought out Ender. He hadn't slept with us in the bed, but he hadn't left either. He'd opted for the couch, saying he needed his space. I'd have to take it as a win.

He sat up, holding Princess to his chest and running his free hand through his hair that hung around him in wild waves. My fingers itched to delve into it and get lost in the tangle. Princess let out a perturbed meow.

"You know Princess doesn't like getting woken up before eight," Ender muttered.

"I'm sorry, baby," I cooed.

She leapt off Ender and hopped onto the bed to headbutt my chin. I giggled and cuddled her to me. "Hi, sweet girl."

Her purrs started like a race car engine.

Puck leaned over, moving to stroke her belly. "You make her all docile—"

The moment Puck's fingers touched the cat's fur, she snarled, biting and kicking his hand.

"Goddammit, Ender! What is wrong with that cat?" Puck yelled.

Ender just burst out laughing. "She has good sense. That's all."

"Be nice, Princess," I chided. The kitty just licked my chin.

"Traitor," Puck muttered.

I glanced at him. "Me or the cat?"

"You," he clipped.

That only made me laugh. "Sorry, buddy."

"Adding insult to injury," he griped.

I stroked under Princess's chin. "Okay, baby. I gotta go get ready."

A series of growls sounded, but it was Brix who spoke. "Where do you think you're going?"

"To the gym. Franco has his bout in three days. This is our last training session."

"I don't know if that's such a good idea," King began.

"Oh, no, you don't," I said, sliding to the end of the bed and putting Princess down. "You're not going to keep me hidden in a tower for the rest of my days. If anything, yesterday should have proven I know how to handle myself."

A muscle fluttered in Kingston's jaw. "I know, but—"

"No. This isn't up for a vote. My life, my choice. And I won't let this bullshit keep me from being a good friend."

"Let her go," Ender said, pushing to his feet. "We'll be with her. And I doubt anyone will make any moves for quite a while. People are shitting their pants that The Diablos found a mate. Some people on the forums are saying supernaturals should move out of Colorado altogether just to be safe."

I shook my head at the pride in his voice. "Feral fucking wolves."

"Don't drop your shoulder," King called from ringside.

"And protect your goddamned face. Your guard is slipping," Clyde snapped.

"Hell," Franco muttered as he circled me. "I'll be glad when this fight is over just so I don't have to listen to those two."

I snickered. "Only if you win. If you lose, you'll never hear the end of it."

Franco groaned. "Dammit, you're right. Save me, Wren."

I laughed, moving in to attempt a double-leg takedown, but Franco was too quick for me this time. He used it as an opening to sweep my legs out from under me. The second my side hit the mat, he dropped and pulled me into an armbar.

I grinned, showing my mouth guard as I tapped the floor in submission. Franco instantly released me and hopped to his feet, offering me a hand.

"Good job," I praised, clapping him on the shoulder.

"Finally," Juan called from the sidelines. "Only took you three years to best her."

I chuckled as Franco flipped off his friend. Pulling out my mouth guard, I slipped between the ropes and jumped down. Puck offered me my mouth guard case while Locke handed me a water bottle. Brix and Ender just stared at me with their arms crossed.

"You let him have that one," Ender clipped. "Even not using your shifter abilities."

"Shut up," I hissed, glancing over my shoulder. But Franco was huddled with King and Clyde, getting last-minute tips. "What he needs going into Saturday is confidence. So that's what I gave him."

Brix's expression softened as he reached for me, pulled me to him, and pressed a kiss to the top of my head. "You're a good friend."

"Should've kicked his ass," Ender muttered.

I couldn't help but laugh.

"So, what time are we meeting up on Saturday?" Juan called, sauntering over. "I'm thinking a little pregame at Arcane."

I pinned him with a hard look. "No getting wasted before the fight even starts. Save it for the celebration after. We can meet there at seven, right?" I suggested, turning to the guys.

I was met with thunderous stares.

"You think going to an MMA fight when you have a bunch of heat on you is a good idea?" Ender snarled.

"Oh, no, you don't, Mr. Pussy Palace," I snapped.

Juan leaned over to Locke. "Did she just say pussy palace?"

"I haven't fought this hard to stay alive to not truly live. I am going to that fight. Whether you come with me is your choice."

Ender glared at me. "Oh, I'm going with you. And I'm going to tear out the eyes of anyone who even looks at you twice."

Juan winced. "Note to self, wear shades to the fight."

CHAPTER FORTY-FOUR

Brix

I STARED INTO THE NIGHT, WATCHING FOR MOVEMENT OR THE flicker of anything that didn't belong. But all I'd seen so far were a family of raccoons and a bat in the distance.

My back teeth ground together, and my fingers itched for my tattoo gun, wanting to mark my skin and take the edge off whatever this foreign feeling coursing through me was. *Worry.* It wasn't something I was used to.

It was as if my whole being was coming alive again after decades of being in hibernation or frozen in stasis. It had hurt like hell coming back, but even after getting past the agony, I had this low-level discomfort coursing through me. I was twitchy. On edge. And not a damn thing seemed to help, other than losing myself in Wren. But, even there, the effects were fleeting.

"Want to tell me why you're glaring at that tree like it stole your last french fry?"

Wren's voice cut through the night like a sultry promise and a warm comfort all at once. She rounded my chair and lowered herself onto my lap, brushing the hair out of my face. The feel of her fingers skating over my skin helped. But not nearly enough.

I stared down at her, trying to take in all her beauty, the wonder of everything she was. "You should be in bed."

Wren arched a brow at me. "Should I?"

"The guys probably miss you."

Her brow furrowed as she tried to read what was beneath my words. "Ender's out patrolling, King's on the phone with the gods only know who, and Locke and Puck are currently in a video game battle to end all video game battles."

We all found our ways to cope, I guessed. Every last one of us was worried about Wren. Terrified that the idiots trying to make a quick buck wouldn't heed King's warning. Or worse, that Bastian would find some new approach to try.

Wren's fingers skimmed over my face, one stopping to trace the knife by my eye. "Want to tell me what's going on?"

No, I didn't. I wasn't someone who talked about my feelings because I wasn't used to having them. But it wasn't fair to lock her out.

"Feel twitchy," I admitted.

I thought Wren would push to know the emotional reason behind that twitchiness, but she didn't. Instead, she simply asked, "What do you normally do when you feel this way?"

"Ink."

Two adorable wrinkles formed on her brow. "Ink?"

"I usually tattoo myself, but if you haven't noticed, I'm running out of space."

"Oh." Wren's mouth formed a perfect circle that had me thinking of other things. Then, something shifted in her expression. "What if you tattoo me?"

A new sensation slid over me—a buzz of adrenaline, attraction, and excitement, but there was a hint of doubt in the stew, too. "You sure that's a good idea? I've seen your body. There's not a speck of ink on it."

Wren shrugged. "No time like the present to start."

I studied her, one corner of my mouth kicking up. "As easy as that?"

"Why not? I trust you."

Fuck.

That did something to me, this magnificent creature gifting me her trust. If I didn't ink her, I'd fuck her instead. But for now, I'd mark her in a whole other way.

In one swift move, I stood and tossed Wren over my shoulder. She squealed. "Brix!"

My palm came down hard on her ass, making her wiggle. "Quiet. I don't want any of these other assholes ruining my fun."

Wren bit my back playfully. "I'm going to get you back for this. You could've let me walk."

"Whatever punishment you dole out will be worth it."

"You say that now…"

I chuckled as I navigated the maze of hallways until we reached the small tattoo studio Ender and I kept at the house. It was where we inked the guys and ourselves. Tattooing supernaturals was different than humans. It required special enchanted ink, and the healing was practically instantaneous. But the process was also a bit more painful. Which was part of why I liked it.

Flicking on the lights, I closed the door behind us and set Wren on the tattoo bed in the center of the room. She landed with an oomph and glared up at me.

"Hey," I said, my lips twitching. "Most people would just say thank you for the lift."

"Gee, thanks."

I chuckled, moving around the room to get set up.

"I really need to get better acquainted with this house. I had no idea this was even here," Wren said as she studied the framed artwork on the wall made up of mostly my and Ender's designs.

"It's tucked away. Just how I like it."

I felt Wren's eyes on me more than I saw them. Her attention had a warmth to it. But it probed, too—not forcefully or harshly, but in a way that said she wanted to know more.

She didn't disappoint. "Why do you hide what's clearly a gift?"

"It's not for other people. It's for me," I told her honestly.

"It's how you process," Wren surmised.

I nodded as I washed my hands and donned gloves. "The pain has always been an outlet. The beauty left behind is proof that I made it through."

"You hurt yourself to deal with whatever's going on in your head."

"That makes it sound twisted."

"Isn't it just a little twisted?" she asked quietly.

"Maybe. But so am I."

Grief passed over Wren's expression. "And tonight, you need to deal because you're worried about me."

It wasn't a question, but I still felt the need to answer. "I'm not used to fearing for someone other than me."

"Not even your brothers?"

I shook my head. "I've always just known they'll take care of themselves."

Heat flashed in Wren's blue eyes. "I can take care of myself."

"I know you can. But it's different. You're a part of me. You're my soul's mate. The urge to protect you…it's like it drowns out everything else."

She frowned and then pushed up the hem of her shorts on one leg. "Then let me help you deal. Let me take the pain."

CHAPTER FORTY-FIVE

Wren

What Brix didn't understand was that his pain was already a living, breathing thing to me. I could feel it raking against my skin, clawing at my heart. And it was worse because I loved him. Because he was my mate.

But wasn't that the burden of love? You got all the wonderful things: connection, passion, understanding. But it also meant that you hurt when the person you loved did. It was just amplified for me because of my empathic gift.

Only I couldn't find it in me to regret it. Not even as smoky tendrils of Brix's pain tried to grab me and put me in a vicious stranglehold. Because what would have happened if I wasn't here? Would Brix have been left to deal with it himself?

If so, I understood why he'd turned it all off. It was too much for anyone to bear alone.

"No." The word was low and a little angry as it tore from Brix's throat. "It's my pain. It's not for you to take."

I stared up at him as he stood there, some tattoo device I couldn't identify in his hands. "And you don't take on my pain? You help me fight back my nightmares. You protect me with everything you have. You listen and truly hear."

A muscle fluttered in Brix's cheek. "It's not the same. I'm too dark."

"You're not." I reached out, needing more connection. I gripped his black tee with faded *Arcane* lettering and tugged him to me. "You're scarred. Just like me." I slipped my hand under the soft cotton, feeling for his marked flesh, the twisted skin covered by the ink. "It's how we understand each other so deeply. And I'd pay those prices over and over if it meant finding you in the end."

"Little Warrior," he growled.

I took a little of his darkness into me then, making his pain mine.

"Don't."

"It's mine, the same as you are," I whispered.

A different sort of pain flashed across his face. "Enough."

Slowly, I pulled my hand away from his skin, knowing I'd taken the edge off. Just enough for him to see a little more clearly. But I asked for something more. "Mark me. Paint our tether in a way I'll see it every day."

"Wren—"

"I love you," I said, cupping his face with my hands. "I feel it. I see it in our mark here." I pressed a hand to my shoulder. "I want to see your art on me, too. I want to feel that piece of you with me."

Brix studied me for a long moment, his head tilting to the side as it often did when he was trying to think something through. "You don't want to tell me what to ink on your skin forever?"

I released my hold on his face and lay back on the bed that resembled a massage table. "I told you. I trust you." I closed my eyes to punctuate the point. I wouldn't look until he was done.

Brix didn't move at first. I counted to almost one hundred

before I felt cool liquid being swept across my thigh. My mouth curved in response. And then a buzz lit the air.

"Tell me if it's too much," Brix said, his voice low.

"I will." I wouldn't. I'd already walked through fire. This would be nothing.

When the needle bit into my skin, I had to bite back a curse. The pain took my breath away for a second but then shifted into something different. A heady heat. I could see why this was a release for Brix.

I let all the darkness in me swirl and pictured it bleeding out of my skin, becoming one with the ink. I lost all sense of time as Brix worked. The buzzing pain mixed with release and Brix wiping away what I assumed was blood and ink.

When the buzzing cut off this time, it didn't start back up.

"Done," Brix rasped.

My eyelids fluttered, light shining through in quick bursts. Brix held out a hand, and I took it. He helped me sit up, and I viewed my thigh. The most beautiful artwork I'd ever seen now graced the tan and marred flesh.

It only took me a second to recognize my wolf—her dark-brown fur with the patch of white. Wrapped around her was a jet-black wolf. Brix. It was a protective pose, but he didn't stand in front of her. He was a show of force at her back. Throughout the artwork were tiny silvery starbursts.

"They're the shards of feeling coming back," Brix explained, pointing to one.

I leaned forward and brushed my lips against his. "It's the most beautiful gift I've ever received."

Brix's mouth curved against mine. "I've never felt what I did when I inked your skin. Everything is…more."

"I hope it was a good more because I think I'm going to want you to do that again."

Brix laughed and helped me down, steadying me for a moment. "A very good more. You might want to shower and get the remnants off your skin. It's not like a human tattoo; it's already fully healed."

I grinned up at him. "Want to help me?"

Brix let out a low growl and then cursed. "I have to go on patrol. Ender will probably be back by now."

It was my turn to curse this time. "Gonna make you pay for leaving me high and dry."

Heat filled Brix's eyes as his hand fisted my hair. "I certainly hope so."

I scowled at him as I turned to leave. Walking away felt like torture, but I forced myself to do it anyway. As I wound through the maze back toward the center of the house, I heard sounds of sparring coming from the gym. I couldn't help my curiosity and poked my head in to see who was getting in a late-night workout. I promptly stopped dead.

Ender and King sparred with bo staffs, both shirtless in low-slung black joggers. They moved around the fighting ring like it was a choreographed dance. Ender had his brown hair pulled up into a man bun, exposing the shaved sides, while King's almost black hair was damp with sweat. And both were covered in ink that I now had a whole new appreciation for.

Pressure built between my thighs, need rushing in with it. I muttered a curse. I needed to get out of here and fast. Because the last people I needed to let my horny she-wolf out around were Kingston and Ender. King because we needed to take things slow, and Ender because, even though we'd reached more of an understanding, he was still most definitely an asshole.

CHAPTER FORTY-SIX

Ender

My bo staff slammed into King's with enough force to make my bones rattle and spine jar. If the staff hadn't been specially made for supernaturals, it would've splintered at the first hit. But even the bite of pain at the contact wasn't enough. It felt like I'd need someone to slice me open and remove an organ to put a dent in the anger and frustration swirling through me at the moment.

And if I was honest, the frustration had a distinctively *sexual* undercurrent.

As if just admitting that had conjured her out of nothing, a hint of Wren's scent teased my nose. I didn't even avert my gaze, but it was enough of a distraction that my guard slipped for just a second. King's bo smacked me right across the face.

"Fucking hell," I snarled, cupping my nose.

"Shit," King muttered. "Is it broken?"

"Yes," I barked, but the word was slightly muffled. I grabbed my nose and snapped it back into place, cursing up a blue streak.

King leaned against his bo staff, studying me. "Not like you to drop your guard."

"Shouldn't you be apologizing for breaking my fucking nose?"

He shrugged like the asshole didn't have a care in the world. "You dropped your guard."

I let out a snarl, putting my bo back on the rack and grabbing my water to wash down the taste of blood in the back of my throat.

"It's almost like something distracted you," King said.

"Fucking wildflowers and rain," I muttered under my breath. The problem was, we were shifters, so King damn well heard every word I said.

A grin spread across his face. "I knew it. You're so gone for her."

"I am not," I snapped.

King's lips twitched. "Keep telling yourself that. Your nose says otherwise."

"Bugger off," I clipped, flipping King the bird as I stalked out of the gym.

"You don't have the adorable accent to pull that off," he called after me.

Whatever.

I stalked down the hallway, not even realizing what my wolf was doing until it was too late. *Following Wren's scent.* By the time I figured it out, I was at the edge of the guestroom that belonged to her. She still had most of her belongings down here. We all needed a space that was ours alone, just like we needed somewhere that was ours to come together. The only problem was that I could hear water running in Wren's room.

But that didn't stop me. My wolf had the reins now, and he wanted his little kitten. The one with the wildflowers-and-rain scent. I pushed her door open and headed for the bathroom.

Wren was everywhere here. It was like her scent was burned into the floor, the furniture, the air itself. But none of that was anything compared to what I saw when I reached the bathroom door. It wasn't open wide, just cracked four or five inches. But through the sliver, I saw a massive mirror that reflected the shower.

Gods, she was the kind of beauty I'd never seen before.

All tan skin, slick with water. Honed muscle and endless curves. Her head tipped back, exposing her throat as the stream surrounded her and the spray doused her mahogany hair.

Water sluiced down her body in rivulets I wanted to trace with my tongue. Her back arched, her nipples pebbled, and that's when I saw her hand.

Those clever fingers darted between her thighs. Her mouth fell open as she sucked in a breath, her cheeks pinking.

Fuck me.

My dick stiffened, pressing against the cotton of my boxer briefs. Even my damn cock was battling to get to her.

Wren's eyes opened, her head tipping back down, and those eyes sparked silver as they caught my gaze in the mirror. She froze.

"Don't stop on my account, Kitten. I'm rather enjoying the show."

More silver fire, spurred on by anger mixing with the heat. "Is that so?"

"Tell me how that pussy feels."

Defiance lit her gaze. "You're the pussy expert. Shouldn't you tell me?"

Little minx. My palm twitched, wanting to bend her over my knee and spank that pert, perfect ass. "Looks to me like you were struggling to make yourself come."

"You could always lend a hand," Wren shot back with a smirk.

"Hand between those thighs, Kitten."

Her lips parted, her nipples pebbling. *Interesting.* My mate liked to be ordered around.

"Ask nicely," she gritted out.

"Please, Kitten," I said, dropping my voice to a husky rasp.

"Slide two fingers into that warm, tight cunt and tell me how good it feels."

Wren whispered a curse but did as I asked, those fingers disappearing inside her—somewhere I desperately wanted to be.

"Tell me," I growled.

Her fingers began gliding in and out, her breaths coming quicker. "Good. But not as good as if it were your fingers."

Damn her. She knew how to torture a man. And enjoyed it, given the little smirk on her lips.

"Palm your breast with your other hand and trace your nipple. Make it hard enough to cut glass."

Wren's hand lifted, and she cupped her perfect tit, fingers gliding over the wet skin.

"That's a good girl. So obedient."

Those blue eyes turned silver again, reminding me that my kitten had claws.

"Add a third finger," I ordered.

She hesitated, trying to decide whether she wanted to play my game.

"Come on. It'll feel so good. Not as good as when I'm stretching you, but you'll have to take what you can get."

Pure liquid fire shot at me through the mirror as Wren's gaze hit white-hot fury. Then she smiled. I should've wondered why, but like an idiot, I didn't.

She lowered herself to the bench in the shower and spread her legs wide. "I think I'd rather play with my clit awhile, if it's all the same to you."

A million curses spilled free as Wren showed me everything I wanted but couldn't have. And I stood frozen, locked in her thrall as she stroked herself with one hand and fucked herself with the other.

Her moans were pleasure and pain, the worst kind of torture, and I deserved every ounce. Wren's chest heaved as her thighs began to shake, then her whole body convulsed, her pleasure evident in every micro expression.

She collapsed against the shower wall, heaving. "I gotta thank you, Cat Daddy. I haven't come that hard on my own in quite a while."

Another round of curses slipped free as I stalked out of the bathroom. I was the one who needed a shower now, but mine needed to be ice-cold.

CHAPTER FORTY-SEVEN

Wren

I CINCHED THE BLACK TOP AND TOOK A STEP BACK TO SURVEY my appearance. At some point in the past few weeks, additional clothes had begun appearing in my closet. None of the guys ever said anything about them, and I'd had too much going on to argue with them about it. Plus, the workout gear was freaking awesome.

Now, I was happy as hell that my mystery benefactor had been at work because I had something new to wear to Franco's fight. But the outfit meant there would be no hiding for me tonight. The top was far more risqué than I'd ever dared to wear before.

But it made me feel powerful, sexy, and strong. There was no disguising the scars that decorated my arms and torso, but it also meant that my mate marks from Brix, Locke, and Puck were on display. The corset pushed up my breasts, and the material below them was a somewhat see-through mesh.

I'd paired the top with black jeans that had artful tatters and tears throughout, including one that allowed my new tattoo to peek out. But on my feet were combat boots. Together, the outfit felt like the perfect mix of old and new. Of finding who I was always meant to be.

A soft knock sounded on my bedroom door, and I stepped out of the closet just as Locke appeared. He froze, his mouth dropping open and his eyes sparking with silver. "Wren," he croaked.

I worried the inside of my cheek. "Too much?"

"Fuck, no," he growled, stepping into my space and pulling me against him. His fingers tangled in my dark hair, tugging on one of the strands I'd curled into loose, sexy waves. "You're the most stunning creature I've ever seen."

"Thanks," I whispered. "I feel…good."

Locke's expression softened, and he skimmed his lips along my neck until he reached his brand, placing a kiss there.

"We gotta go," Puck called from somewhere else in the house. "No fucking till later."

A laugh startled out of me as Locke let out a low growl.

"He's such a cockblock," Locke muttered.

"Come on," I said, taking Locke's hand and leading him to the door. "I don't want to miss Franco's fight."

We made our way toward the front door, where everyone else was waiting. They all went silent the moment I stepped into the light, four sets of eyes pinning me to the spot.

Ender muttered a curse. "I need another ice-fucking-cold shower."

I tried to cover my laugh with a cough, my skin heating at the memory of our encounter.

"I'm going to kill so many assholes tonight," Brix mumbled.

"Worth it," Puck shot back.

King stepped forward, moving so slow it was almost painful, until he was right in front of me. "You look beautiful, Wren." Then he dipped his head and brushed his lips across the worst visible scar, one right across my collarbone.

I sucked in a breath at the touch, and King slowly lifted his head until his eyes met mine. Then I closed the distance, kissing him ever so softly.

"Thanks for giving me a hard-on when we're about to go into a roomful of dudes," Puck muttered, opening the front door.

This time, I didn't try to cover my laugh. I just grinned at Puck as I headed out the door. "Sorry, not sorry, buddy."

Hard rock pulsed through the arena's speakers. It was a full house tonight, and my guys were sticking close.

"Here you go," King said, handing me a whiskey.

I took it from him, our fingers brushing. Then I downed it in two gulps.

"Fuck, that was hot," Puck mumbled.

"Easy, Kitten," Ender warned.

"I'm good," I assured him. I had no plans to get drunk. I just needed a little liquid courage to deal with the crowd of unknowns. But it was worth it. I needed to have a life worth fighting for.

"Ten minutes in the main ring," a voice said over the speakers. "Franco Rossi and Gabe Jackson."

A buzz of excitement surged in my veins, and I scanned our surroundings. "I'm going to find a bathroom before it starts."

King's eyes went alert. "Puck, Locke, you're with Wren. The rest of us will find our seats and do a sweep."

None of them were drinking. I understood why, but what I wanted more than anything was a night where we didn't have to worry about having all our faculties. A night where we could be free.

I glanced at Puck and Locke. "Come on, bodyguards. Let's make this quick."

The crowd was predominantly male, so I hoped there wasn't a super long line for the bathroom. The three of us made our way down a crowded hall to two restrooms. Puck snarled at any dude who gave me a once-over, and Locke walked so closely behind me that I almost tripped.

We came to a stop in front of the ladies' room. "I'll be quick," I said.

"We'll be here," Locke promised.

Pushing the door open, I stepped inside. I quickly did my business and rounded a corner to the sinks to wash my hands, letting the chatter of other women swirl around me. As I dried my hands, the room went silent. Too silent.

I lifted my head to check, but it was too late. A hand fisted in my hair and yanked hard. And then I was tumbling backward.

CHAPTER FORTY-EIGHT

Puck

I TAPPED MY FOOT ON THE LINOLEUM OF THE HALLWAY, MY gaze sweeping over the endless array of humans and the occasional supernatural milling about. Normally, I loved fight night. The buzz of energy in the air, the infectious adrenaline. But now, all I could see were potential risks.

The scent of a vampire teased my nose, and my canines pressed against my gums in response. Vampires and wolves were rarely friends, and knowing one was near Wren had my hackles rising. But as I looked at all the humans in the hall, I knew that any of them could be dangerous. Bastian could've paid someone off or used black magic to control them.

"Fuck," I muttered.

Locke glanced over at me. "I hate it, too."

"Is it always going to be like this? This brutal panic every time she's away from us?"

Locke's gaze flicked to the bathroom door. "The fresh mating bond makes it worse."

Logically, I knew that. We'd been taught about the different effects mating bonds could have. When they were new, wolves could be extra territorial and protective. But this was pure torture.

"She's taking too long," I gritted out.

"There might be a line inside," Locke reminded me.

"I don't like it."

Locke's lips twitched, but that hint of a smile dropped fast. We both froze. A human wouldn't have heard it, but we weren't humans. Our shifter hearing meant that we picked up on the grunt and answering shriek from the bathroom.

"What the hell?" I snarled.

But Locke was already moving, tearing open the bathroom door and storming inside. I was right behind him. I didn't see a damn thing by the stalls except for a girl gaping at us as she stepped out. "This is the women's room," she snapped.

"When you gotta go, you gotta go," I shot back, stalking around the corner toward the growing sounds of a struggle.

"You broke my nose," a woman wailed—one with a familiar voice.

As Locke and I rounded the corner, we found Dara crumpled on the floor, clutching her face, her brown hair soaking wet.

"My outfit is *ruined*," Siena cried, her blond hair also completely soaked.

But Wren and Cressida were in the center of the bathroom. Cress screamed like a wild banshee, running at Wren with her fists raised. Wren simply sidestepped her at the last moment and stuck out her foot to trip the woman. She caught Cress by the hair as the woman howled.

"You man-stealing bitch!" Cressida screamed. "You're going to pay for this!"

Wren wasn't fazed. She pulled Cressida's arm behind her to

keep her from striking out, then forced her into another set of stalls on our side of the bathroom.

Cress let out a scream, and then we heard a flush. A second later, the redhead flew out of the stall like a kitten who'd fallen into a full bathtub.

Cressida flung her wet hair over her shoulder and glared at Wren. "I'm going to kill you!"

"Oh, you can try. Just like you tried to get the jump on me with your little bitch crew here. But you'll fail at that, too."

Cress let out another battle cry, running full speed at Wren. But it was a mistake. When Cressida was about a foot away, Wren snapped out with a jab to the cheekbone. Cress went down like a puppet whose strings had been cut. Out cold.

The only sounds were those of Dara and Siena, whimpering now. I looked from them to Cressida to Wren, gaping. "Did you give them…swirlies?"

Wren shrugged and straightened her corset. "Bullies should get the bully treatment."

Dara started crying in the corner, going on about how she'd never get clean.

Locke's expression was a little less amused than mine. "They tried to hurt you?" he gritted out.

"*Tried* is the operative word there. Cressida grabbed my hair, and Dara tried to hit me. She missed."

A grin spread across my face. "And you broke her nose."

"It's only fair," Wren said, returning my smile.

"I'm gonna need plastic surgery," Dara wailed.

Wren scowled at her. "No amount of plastic surgery will make your soul pretty."

Dara gaped at her, still holding her nose. "You-you think my soul's ugly?"

"Take a good look in the mirror, lady," Wren snapped.

I couldn't help it, I laughed. "I love the hell out of you."

Wren's expression went soft as she turned back to me. "I love you, too, buddy."

My eyes narrowed. "Do not call me buddy."

She crossed to me and brushed her lips across mine. "Even when I'm telling you I love you?"

I wavered a little, and Wren smelled victory.

"I knew you liked it, buddy."

Locke choked on a laugh, and Wren tugged him to us, kissing him hard.

"I love you, too."

Locke smiled against her mouth. "I know. It's kind of fun to watch you kick some ass."

I glared at the women crumpled on the floor. "But you're all eighty-sixed for life."

A new round of wails sounded.

Wren shot me a huge grin. "That was very satisfying, buddy."

"You're welcome," I said, kissing her quickly.

A new voice sounded, one I recognized from the stalls on the other side of the bathroom. "I don't know what you people are into, but I dig it."

Wren released Locke and me, then crossed to the woman to give her a high five. "I highly recommend swirlying your enemies and finding five loves of your life."

The stranger's jaw dropped. "*Five*?"

Wren nodded, smiling wide. "Five is the perfect number."

"Shit," she mumbled. "I gotta start collecting."

"Good luck," Wren called, moving toward the door.

Locke and I hurried to follow, grinning like the lovesick fools we were.

CHAPTER FORTY-NINE

Wren

I couldn't help the ridiculous, face-cracking smile that stayed etched on my face as we made our way through the crowd, Puck in front of me, and Locke behind.

No more hiding.

And that included no more taking shit from a crew of women who'd never grown out of the high school mean-girl phase. I was done taking cruelty I didn't deserve. From *anyone*. And, gods, that felt good.

Puck maneuvered us toward the front row, where Juan, Clyde, Dina, and the rest of the guys were waiting. Ender's gaze zeroed in on me, his brow furrowing. "She's smiling. Why is she smiling so big?"

Puck chuckled. "Because she just gave Siena, Dara, and Cressida swirlies in the bathroom."

Brix's face scrunched like he'd smelled something bad. "Did you say swirlies?"

"Don't forget the broken nose and the black eye," I added cheerfully.

"What. Happened?" Kingston ground out.

I patted his chest. "Don't worry, alpha man. I'm fine. They tried to start shit. I finished it."

Clyde held out his fist for a bump. "That's how we do."

"Damn straight," I said, touching my knuckles to his.

Dina sighed and looked at Puck. "Tell me you banned them. I do not want to have to deal with their whiny selves come Monday."

"Eighty-sixed for life," Puck promised.

Dina held her hands in the air. "Hallelujah."

I couldn't help the laugh that bubbled from my lips. "Happy to be of service."

Franco moved to the side of the ring, and Clyde ambled up to him. "You ready?" Clyde asked.

Franco jerked his head in a nod, holding his mouth guard in his hand. "Ready."

There was no carefree amusement in him now. Franco was in the zone. The same couldn't be said for Juan.

"You got this, beast man. Think about all the pussy you're gonna get when you demolish his ass."

Clyde scowled at Juan. "Don't make me deck you."

"What? What'd I say?" Juan asked, fighting a grin.

I just shook my head, turning to find my seat. But behind my chair was a man whose neck was as thick as a bodybuilder's thigh, and his gaze roamed over me in a way that did not give me the warm fuzzies.

"Girl, you look good. After this fight, how 'bout I take you for a ride?" he said, his tongue running over his lower lip.

I had to fight the urge to gag. But before I could say anything, Brix stepped in front of me, his alpha vibes filling the air. Humans didn't know what the energy was, but it still affected them. Mostly resulting in piss-your-pants fear.

"How about you find another seat, and I don't remove your head from your body?" Brix snarled.

The man blanched. "I-I paid triple for the VIP seats."

Brix bared his teeth at the man. "Move or lose a limb."

The man scampered, moving quicker than a person his size should be able to.

"B," I cajoled. "That wasn't nice."

Brix let out a chuff that sounded more animal than human. "He's lucky he's still breathing."

I moved into my protector, pressing my lips to his cheek. "No removing limbs or organs tonight, okay?"

"I can't make any promises," Brix grumbled.

"Ladies and gentlemen," the ref said, stepping forward. "The main fight is about to begin."

Cheers went up, and the buzz of anticipation filled the air. I couldn't make myself sit. Too many nerves swirled inside me as Franco stepped into the center of the ring. His opponent let out a snarl that almost seemed wolf-like, even though I knew Gabe Jackson had no shifter blood.

The ref glanced at both men. "I want a good, clean fight. Touch gloves, then back to your corners."

Franco's expression was blank as Gabe snarled and spittle flew. But the men touched gloves and retreated. A second later, the bell sounded.

Gabe didn't wait. He attempted to use the element of surprise and take Franco to the mat. I understood why. Gabe was known for his grappling skills. If he could get Franco on the ground, his chances of winning were much greater.

But Franco had the speed. Those hours of running with weighted vests and jumping rope in the gym paid off as he easily dodged Gabe's attempt at a takedown.

The two men circled each other, throwing out the occasional testing jab, but no one got a solid hit in. Then Gabe surprised

Franco with a hook to the jaw. Franco blocked some of it, but Gabe's fist still connected.

The crowd roared with a combination of boos and cheers.

"Come on, Franco," I yelled. "Guard up. Make him play your game."

Franco rolled to the balls of his feet, leaning forward and making Gabe think he was going for a jab. But then Franco used that speed he'd trained for, ducked low, and threw an uppercut to the ribs instead.

Gabe stumbled back a step, and Franco followed up with a hook to the jaw. The crowd went wild as the judges scrawled down marks on their score sheets.

But Gabe wasn't done. He let out a roar and sent a one-two combo into Franco's face.

I cursed as Franco nearly lost his footing, blood streaming from his nose. "You've got this, Franco. Take him down!"

Franco let the force of the blow tip him sideways but used the energy to pull off a side kick that landed squarely in Gabe's ribs. He crumpled, bending forward and trying to suck in a breath. But he used that energy, too, diving for Franco's legs.

The two men hit the mat with deafening force, and I couldn't breathe. My hands fisted, knowing this was exactly what Gabe had wanted: a grappling match where he could dominate.

Except Franco was quick. He grabbed Gabe's head in a guillotine choke hold, making the man's face turn bright red as he tried to wriggle out of it. He threw punch after punch into Franco's side.

But Franco didn't budge. He wrapped his legs around Gabe, strangling his whole body.

Gabe started to weaken but didn't make any move to give up.

His coach yelled orders ringside, but the man showed no signs of listening. "Tap the fuck out," the coach screamed.

Gabe didn't give the two touches required to do so. Franco held steady until Gabe's entire body went limp. The ref moved in as fast as lightning, slicing his hands through the air. "TKO!"

The crowd erupted. I jumped up, King catching me as we all screamed for our friend and his victory.

Gabe slowly came around and was able to stand, scowling as the ref lifted Franco's hand in the air.

We hooted and hollered, and I didn't think I'd ever felt happier than in that moment. It was more than winning. It was knowing everything Franco had put into the bout. Being a part of that journey with the men I loved. And getting to do this *life* together.

CHAPTER FIFTY

Wren

Music blared from the speakers at Arcane, old-school rock that had people singing along or heading for the makeshift dance floor. We weren't officially open, but we might as well have been. The man of the hour was nursing a beer, his arm around his new girlfriend. Plenty of folks from the gym dotted tables and stools at the bar, along with their partners or people they'd brought along for the celebration.

My mouth curved as I watched Clyde pull Dina out onto the dance floor. She blushed as he spun her into his arms.

"Interesting," Puck said, dropping his chin to my shoulder as we studied the pair. "Does love bloom eternal?"

I chuckled. "Maybe. I can see the two of them together. She keeps him on his toes."

Puck straightened, spinning my stool and stepping between my legs. "Happy?"

"The happiest." My hand fisted in his tee, and I pulled his mouth to mine.

Puck kissed me with a mix of heat and comfort, his tongue stroking in. I moaned into his mouth, and he pulled me closer.

A catcall sounded, making me pull back and send a glare in Juan's direction. He held up both hands in surrender. "What? I can't appreciate a friend getting herself some?"

Kingston smacked him upside the head. "Stop being an idiot."

Juan laughed, jogging off in search of either liquor or a lady friend.

King strode over to us, a gentle smile on his face. "Thanks for making us do this."

"Hey, I didn't force anyone."

One corner of King's mouth tugged up. "You know we'll do anything to keep you safe."

I threaded my fingers through his, squeezing gently. "I just don't want us to lose sight of what we're fighting for."

I scanned the room, taking in my friends, both old and new. Nothing about the night was over-the-top. It was simple but filled with so much joy.

King dipped his head and pressed a kiss to my temple. "You reminded us. And I think we needed an excuse to let loose a little."

An older woman tried to pull Locke onto the dance floor, but he shook his head. I couldn't help but laugh at the slight panic in his eyes as he tugged himself free and made a beeline for us. When he saw my face, he scowled. "It's not funny."

"Just a little funny," I argued. "You don't want to dance?"

"She's been following me around, throwing out cheesy pickup lines," Locke groused as he straightened his glasses.

"Don't worry, I'll protect you," I assured him.

"I'm counting on it."

Puck chuckled. "It's those boyish good looks. The ladies love it."

Locke turned his glare on the Brit. "She's old enough to be my grandma."

Puck held up both hands. "I'm not here to judge."

King chuckled. "You need a beer, Locke? Ease the panic?"

"Sure," he mumbled.

King reached behind the bar, grabbed a bottle from a bucket of ice, and handed it to Locke, who popped the top.

"There are too many people in here," Brix muttered as he strode in from the back hallway.

I grinned at him. "Don't be a curmudgeon. We're celebrating."

Brix looked affronted. "I'm not a curmudgeon. It's just loud."

"He might as well be screaming, '*Get off my lawn*,'" King said, amusement lacing his tone.

Brix let out a huff. "Is it so bad that I prefer the quiet of home?"

I patted his shoulder. "No, but it's good for you to get out once in a while. Remember, there's a whole world out here."

"The whole world's stupid," he mumbled.

I laughed, my gaze scanning the room. I didn't know what I was looking for until I landed on him. Ender stood against the far wall, expression stoic and arms crossed. Our eyes locked, and I couldn't look away. He looked so damn lonely.

The emotion snaked out, reaching across the room and grating my skin. But loneliness was an emotion that would always return if the person didn't take steps to remedy it. Even if I took the heaviness into me, I could do nothing to keep it from coming back.

"It's his choice," Brix said softly. "We can't force him to jump. I know he'll do it; he's just taking his sweet-ass time."

I hoped Brix was right. Hoped that Ender was just finding his way toward us. The path might be winding, but it would eventually get there.

I pushed off my stool, forcing the guys to give me room. "Who wants a shot?"

"Oh, shit," Locke muttered.

King leveled me with a stare. "Are you sure that's a good idea?"

"We need to live a little, remember?" But I only made it two steps toward the back of the bar when the sound of glass shattering had me whirling around.

Flames. Some sort of bottle with flames had been thrown through the window. Ender moved, trying to stamp it out, but more windows shattered, explosions sounding around the room. And then there was fire everywhere.

CHAPTER FIFTY-ONE

Locke

AN EXPLOSION SOUNDED, THE NOISE MAKING MY EARS ring.

What the hell? Explosion?

That didn't make sense. It couldn't be happening. I must've been having a nightmare. But the screams around me were far too real. And that's when my analytical brain took over.

I counted. The time between detonations was too exact. This was no accident.

I was moving before I considered the wisdom of it because only one thing mattered right now: Wren.

My body hit hers in a tackle, taking us both to the floor. She wheezed, trying to shake me off, but I wouldn't let her.

"Stay down," I barked. "There are incendiary devices rigged in here."

And there was no way to know where the next one would be. I scanned the room, smoke already filling it, and looked for anything that didn't belong. I wasn't a bomb expert by any means but—*hell.*

"Watch out!" I yelled across the room, seeing a small device between two of the tables. But it was too late.

Just as the words slipped free, another explosion sounded. Franco covered his new girlfriend, protecting her from the blast.

"The humans," Wren rasped. "We have to get them out."

Of course, her thoughts were for everyone but herself. Whether it was her empathic nature or just who Wren was, she always put others first.

"Wait," King ordered, another explosion sounding, taking out the far end of the bar. "We need to wait until the explosions stop."

But I worried it would be too late by then, that the fire would've spread too much. Throwing Molotov cocktails through the windows was one thing, but these explosive devices were something else entirely. Something that took planning, breaking and entering, and a complete disregard for human life.

My gut twisted as the sounds shifted from explosions to fire. The heat in the room was stifling, the smoke so thick it made it hard to see and difficult to breathe.

"We have to get out," someone screamed.

I heard a woman crying and another person calling for help.

"Now," Wren clipped.

I rolled off her, and she struggled to her feet but crouched low, trying to avoid the worst of the smoke. "Should we get people out the back or the front?"

"Front," Ender ordered, joining our huddle. "I managed to shoot it open, but someone tried to bar the door."

Sickness swept through me. Whoever had done this wanted us all to die in here.

I glanced at Ender. "Can you shoot out some of the windows? It'll give the smoke an outlet. That might help."

He jerked his head in a nod, pulled an arrow from his quiver, and nocked it in his bow. I had no idea where the hell he had that stashed in the bar. I was just glad he did. Ender moved, shooting out four small windows up high in rapid-fire succession. Smoke poured out of them, and I just hoped it was enough to help.

"We pair off," Brix said. "No one's alone."

"We get Wren outside first," Puck argued.

"The hell you do," she snapped. "I'm helping until everyone's out."

A series of growls sounded, mine included. She didn't understand how vital she was to our survival. Without her, we'd fade away into nothing.

Wren's jaw clenched, anger making the muscle there twitch. "You can argue, or we can get going."

Brix moved in closer to her. "I'll stick with Wren."

"Ender and Locke, you're together. Puck, you're with me. We move quickly and don't take any unnecessary risks. Go!" King shouted.

End and I crawled toward the sounds of a woman wailing. When we reached her, we saw why. A man I recognized from the gym but didn't know was pinned beneath a wooden beam.

"I can't get him out. You have to help. I-I can't move it," she cried.

Ender wrapped his arms around the beam and glanced at me. "The second I lift, you pull him out."

I coughed but nodded. End gritted his teeth, straining under the weight of the beam I knew had to be a mix of steel and wood. Ender might be a shifter, but this would be heavy for anyone. With a final grunt, he managed to lift the beam enough for me to slide the man out.

Moving as quickly as possible, I lifted him into my arms as the beam crashed to the floor. Ender grabbed the woman, and we took off for the door. The smoke was still so thick I hoped no one noticed our supernatural speed.

Sirens sounded in the distance, and Ender and I ran back inside. We moved to help Franco and his girlfriend next.

"Clyde," Franco rasped, struggling to stand. "Someone has to help Clyde."

"I've got him," Wren yelled through the thick smoke.

Fucking hell.

I wanted her out of here. Safe. This whole building could come down at any moment.

Dipping beneath Franco's arm, I steadied him, helping him to the door. The second we were outside, he collapsed in a coughing fit. Ender set his girlfriend down next to him.

End was already moving back toward the building, and I hurried after him. My lungs felt like they were on fire from the heat and smoke, but I pushed through.

We scoured the room for signs of life.

A moan sounded, and Ender and I instantly headed in that direction. Dina lay crumpled on the floor, blood on her temple. A curse slipped free. Dina. She'd always been so strong and fiery. Seeing her like this was wrong in every way. But I didn't let myself lose it.

Instead, I slipped my arms under her and cradled her against me.

"Follow me," Ender ordered. He led the way, helping me navigate the flames and debris until we reached the door. We spilled out as firefighters aimed hoses at the flames.

My pack mates helped tend wounds and get the worst to the EMTs. But as I scanned the parking lot, I noticed one thing missing.

Panic seared me. "Where's Wren?"

CHAPTER FIFTY-TWO

Wren

SMOKE CLOGGED THE AIR AS SHOUTS SOUNDED FROM outside. The fire department was here. Good. That was good. We just had to get the last few people out.

"Help!"

The word was more croak than scream, but the force behind it told me someone was desperate. I glanced at Brix, but he was already moving in that direction.

I coughed, covering my face with my arm as if that might help protect me from the smoke. I cursed myself for wearing the stupid corset. If I had on my usual T-shirt, I'd at least have something to use as a mask.

Brix and I moved through the rubble, looking for signs of life. I still hadn't seen Clyde and hoped like hell someone had gotten him out. My stomach cramped at the thought of the man who'd become like a father to me being hurt or worse.

"Help." The call was weaker this time. I wasn't sure it

would've been audible to anyone other than shifters, but Brix and I heard it.

We both stilled, looking around. And that's when I saw it. A soot-streaked face peeking out from beneath a pile of rubble. Broken tables. Part of a beam. Who knew what else?

Juan.

I rushed over to him. "Shit, Juan. Are you okay?"

What a stupid question. Of course, he wasn't. I instantly began clearing the detritus piled on top of him.

"You're a sight for sore eyes," he rasped. "I mean, you're always nice to look at, but—" He started coughing, cutting off his words.

"Save the hitting on her for later," Brix said, hurrying to help me clear the rubble.

"But she probably feels bad for me now. I gotta shoot my shot," Juan whispered, his voice fading.

"Gonna tell all the girls at the gym that you fought fire and lived to tell the tale," I said, my eyes filling with tears. "Get ready for all that attention."

"Think…they'll…play…nurse?"

I choked on some combination of a laugh and a sob. "I'm sure they'll be fighting over the costume."

Juan's eyes fluttered. "Good… Did you get Clyde?"

I stiffened, my gaze shooting to Brix. "No. Where is he?"

"Back. Hall. We tried to get out there. Door. Locked."

Fuck. When I found out who'd done this, I was going to relish helping Brix and Ender with their torture.

My hands moved faster, pulling away broken boards from Juan's body. Blood oozed from his shoulder, and I could see where one of his legs was pinned.

"I lift, you pull him out," Brix said.

I jerked my head in a nod. "Then I'm going for Clyde."

"Wren—"

"Lift the damn beam," I clipped.

Brix lifted it, and I slid Juan out, his breathing labored.

"Go!" I yelled, already running for the back hall.

Brix hollered after me, but I didn't stop. I knew he'd do the right thing. He'd get Juan out and then come back and help me.

The smoke thickened in the back hallway, and I fought to breathe, crouching lower. Fire raged in the kitchen, and I struggled to round the entryway without getting burned. Something sounded up ahead. Banging maybe?

I tried to stand, squinting as the smoke cleared. And that's when I saw it. Two firefighters at the end of the hall, and they had Clyde. Relief swept through me.

We were okay. We were going to be okay.

And then one of the firefighters tipped up his mask.

Everything in me stilled. Dark eyes. Hair and nose so similar to mine. But everything about him was pure coldness.

"Bastian," I croaked.

"Little Flower," he cooed. "It could've been so easy. You could've submitted to my authority, and no one would have been hurt. But now you've gone and put everyone in your life at risk."

My breaths came quicker—short, smoke-filled pants that made me cough even harder.

"What about this poor, elderly fool whose only mistake was letting you into his world?" Bastian singsonged as his minion held Clyde in a firm grip. Bastian unsheathed his claws. "I could gut him right here. Should I do that, Little Flower?"

"No!" I cried.

Clyde tried to fight against the enforcer's hold, but he was weak from smoke inhalation.

"You have a choice," Bastian snarled. "You come with me, and he goes free. Or you fight, and you both die here and now. Your head on a spike will serve as a reminder to everyone to *never* disobey me, *never* betray me, and proof that you can *NEVER* escape my wrath."

"Don't," Clyde whispered, his head starting to droop.

Tears filled my eyes as I turned to Bastian. "Let him go. I'll submit."

The words were just out of my mouth when I felt a prick in my neck. I tried to swat it away, but it was too late. I was fading.

And when someone caught me, they said, "I can't wait to make your life a living hell."

CHAPTER FIFTY-THREE

Kingston

SIRENS SCREAMED THROUGH THE NIGHT, SETTING MY WOLF on edge. Who was I kidding? Everything about tonight set my wolf on edge.

Because none of this was an accident. It was a carefully planned attempt to hurt and kill. And whoever had set it into motion hadn't cared about the innocent people caught in the cross fire.

Firefighters aimed hoses at the front of the building, trying their best to battle the flames. But my head was on a swivel, bracing for an attack. Because the moment we'd started to get the humans out, I'd realized that was exactly what we'd set ourselves up for.

It was a common tactic to attempt to weaken before going in for the kill—one that often worked. And all my people were weak at the moment.

I helped a woman hold an oxygen mask to her face as an EMT treated a burn on the man next to us. There weren't enough ambulances to get all the people to the hospital over an hour away, so the sheriff had called in reinforcements from surrounding towns.

So far, no one had been killed, but the night wasn't over, and smoke inhalation could do more damage than you could see right away.

Locke charged across the parking lot, his eyes wild and soot covering his face. "Where's Wren? I don't see her anywhere."

Panic spread through me, and I clambered to my feet, making sure the woman had her oxygen mask. "What about Brix?"

Locke shook his head. "I don't see him either."

I tried to let that knowledge soothe me. Brix had Wren's back. They were fine. "They could still be helping people get out or assisting EMTs with medical care."

Ender's mouth set into a firm line as he and Puck stalked up. "I can't find either of them anywhere. No one else has seen them for a while."

Fuck.

I started toward the building just as a figure emerged from the smoke. Brix struggled with someone in his arms. Normally, carrying a human would be nothing for a shifter, but smoke affected us like everyone else.

Puck ran forward, grabbing the person from Brix's hold as he doubled over and began coughing.

Some part of my brain recognized Juan, barely breathing. Puck shouted for an EMT, and one rushed forward with a gurney. As Puck laid Juan on it, Ender supported Brix. "Are you okay? Where's Wren?"

"Inside," he wheezed. "Helping Clyde."

A fresh wave of panic swept through me as firefighters yelled for people to get back. A horrible cracking and popping sound tore through the air, and I watched in horror as the southwest corner of the building started to crumble.

"Wren." Her name was barely audible on my lips—more prayer than anything else.

I charged for the door, but a firefighter stepped into my path.

"You can't go in there. It's not safe," he barked.

"Someone's still inside. I have to help her," I snarled.

Not just someone. The person who was my everything.

"I'm sorry," the man said. "We'll send firefighters in as soon as we have the blaze under control."

The urge to rip out his jugular was strong. I wanted to toss him aside and run for the door.

"Over here!" a firefighter yelled. "We need medical."

Hope surged. Had Wren gotten out?

I was running before I realized my feet had started moving, heading into the alley along the side of the building that led to the main road through town. I felt the guys behind me, their hope a palpable energy. But the second I saw the figure on the ground, disappointment surged. It was far too large to be Wren.

Slowing, I took in the familiar form. *Clyde.*

The firefighter pressed their fingers to his neck. "Pulse is weak," he shouted at the EMT.

A uniformed woman crouched low, placing an oxygen mask over his face and moving to start an IV.

"Did anyone else get out?" I barked at the firefighter.

The alpha tone bleeding into my words had the man paling slightly, but he shook his head. "I didn't even see him get out. Just found him collapsed in the alley."

I stared at the door, swinging open and closed.

"Don't," the firefighter said, his voice low. "You'll be dead before you get ten steps inside."

So, what did that mean for Wren?

Coughing sounded, pulling my gaze back to Clyde. He struggled, trying to pull his mask down while the EMT fought to keep it in place.

Puck moved in, attempting to shove the EMT out of the way. "He's trying to tell us something."

The EMT glared at him. "He needs oxygen."

"Lady," Ender growled, "if you don't move aside, I'm going to put an arrow in you."

Her jaw went slack, but the shock allowed Clyde to pull down the mask.

"He has her." Clyde's voice was barely audible, but I made out every word.

"Who?" I demanded. Terror and panic striking deep.

"Weird...name...Ba-Bastian."

My brothers and I froze.

"Traded...my...life...for...hers," Clyde wheezed.

Agony and rage ripped through me. Wren had given herself over to save this man. I'd failed her. Hadn't protected her like I'd vowed I always would. And now, she was with the monster of her nightmares.

READ ON FOR A LOOK AT THE EXCITING CONCLUSION TO THE WOLVES OF CRESCENT CREEK SERIES, *RISING REIGN*

CHAPTER ONE

Wren

RAIN PELTED MY SKIN, FEELING LIKE TINY KNIVES SLICING into me. But, still, I tipped my face to the darkening sky. *Water.* I needed this water. Opening my mouth, I caught as many drops on my tongue as possible.

I kept my eyes closed. It was easier that way, trying not to take in the surrounding walls of the pit. The towering way they enclosed me. The occasional snake that made its way down. The countless creepy-crawlies.

Breathe, Wren.

I forced my inhale to slow. No jerky, stuttered breaths that would feed my panic. As I brought the muggy air into my lungs, I scented the bayou water—the thick heaviness of it—and the rotting aromas that seemed to cling to my father's territory.

No. Not my father. Bastian. The bastard who'd taken everything from me.

My back screamed, and the memories of the whip slicing into

my flesh rose. A lash for every month I'd been away. My wolf pressed at my skin, wanting out, wanting to rid the world of every being who had caused us harm.

"With time," I whispered. "With time."

I lifted the shirt that had been given to me after the lashing, letting out a whimper as it peeled away from my blood-caked skin. Keeping my eyes closed, I called on my wolf—not for a full transition, but enough to bring on some healing.

My skin tingled as I felt fur ripple over my limbs, torso, and then my face. My breaths turned into those short pants I was trying to hold off—pain-filled ones—as my knees finally gave way, and I hit the muddy ground with a thud.

The healing was necessary but took far too much energy. Especially when I hadn't been given food or water in at least seventy-two hours. As my fingers dug into the mud, I pictured the guys in my mind. I painted each of their faces in such detail that it felt like I could reach out and touch each one.

A keening noise left my lips, my wolf crying out at being separated from her mates. My human half was just as devastated. Everything in me ached, and it was from more than just the beatings I'd taken. It was a soul-deep pain.

But I kept breathing. For the guys and for myself. I refused to let Bastian Boudreaux win. He wouldn't break me.

I slowly forced my eyes open. It was getting darker, ramping the panic inside me higher. But then I pictured Locke—the way he held me and soothed my touch-hunger, how his voice sounded with his gentle reassurances—and the panic eased a fraction.

Leaning back on my heels, I studied my surroundings: mud and stone held in place by what looked like heavy-duty chicken wire or something similar. It was the only thing keeping the pit from collapsing since it was so close to the water.

The rain eased a bit, but as it did, a shiver racked me. *Not a good sign.* My shifter nature should've protected me from the cold. If it wasn't, my energy stores were running on empty.

I didn't let the fear of that realization in. I let logic reign. Because Bastian didn't want me dead. Not yet, anyway. He wanted me to feel every ounce of pain that he and his minions dished out.

A shudder ran through me at the memory of Marcelle's snarling face as he took his turn with the whip. The way he'd grabbed my hair afterward and whispered, *"Just wait until you're in heat. I'm going to make you pay in ways your nightmares can't even imagine."*

Breathe, Wren. Just breathe.

This time, I pictured Kingston. The way his callused hands felt as they framed my face. How he promised that everything would be okay and made it so. The sweet, thoughtful gifts he left for me to find.

My panic eased again. Because the guys were my talismans, my guiding lights. And I would find my way back to them.

Footsteps sounded in the distance, and I instantly launched to my feet, every muscle and limb crying out in protest. I might've healed myself, but that sort of pain lived on like an echo you couldn't wash away.

I tipped my head back, watching, waiting, listening. The steps were heavy, likely male, and carried anger.

Steeling myself, I tapped into my empath gift ever so slightly.

Pure darkness slammed into me, making me stumble. I instantly threw up my walls, but the darkness still slid inside. Nausea rolled through me as sheer agony raged.

Then, a face appeared over the side of the pit, and Marcelle sneered. "Enjoying being back where you belong, bitch?"

I struggled to pull air into my lungs. The rotting bayou scents of the Red River and Marcelle's stomach-turning stench filled my nose.

"Nothing to say?" he snarled. "Good. I like my women silent and obedient. You'll be trained as such."

I nearly vomited then but managed to keep a hold of myself. Losing any water from my system now could be catastrophic.

Marcelle threw a rope ladder down, and I scurried to get out of its path.

"That's it. Run, little bitch."

I bit the inside of my cheek to hold back my retort as the ladder clattered against the side of the pit.

"Start climbing. Your father wants to see you."

It took everything in me to hold back my shudder. I didn't want to give Marcelle or Bastian the satisfaction. Instead, I began to climb.

I'd tried refusing as a child, curled into a ball at the bottom of the pit, and hoping for death. Instead, I'd gotten the worst beating of my life. Then Bastian had brought a healer to fix me, only to do it all over again. I'd learned to never refuse.

But something about choosing to climb to my own punishment was even more painful. It made me feel weak and pathetic.

"You're strong," I whispered to myself. "You survive. That's what matters."

"What'd you say, little bitch?" Marcelle snapped.

I didn't answer. Instead, I pictured Brix in my mind. The way he'd shielded himself and his emotions for so long. How strong he'd been through his pain. And the way he'd let me in—the gift that was. If he could make it through, so could I.

My entire body cried out in pain as I climbed. Muscle. Skin. Bones. Everything felt like it was a second away from irrevocably breaking.

"Faster," Marcelle demanded.

I tried. My muscles screamed, but I pushed harder. The second I was within arm's reach, he grabbed me by the hair, dragged me out, and threw me to the ground. I slid through the mud like some disgusting Slip 'N Slide.

Marcelle's nose flared. "You stink."

No shit, Sherlock.

I refrained from giving voice to that thought. But whose fault was it that I smelled? It wasn't as if they'd given me access to a shower.

"Get up," he barked.

I struggled to my feet, my muscles quaking.

Marcelle was on me in two long strides, grabbing me by the hair again. "Start walking."

I did as I was ordered. The pit was on the outskirts of the pack territory, with small cabins belonging to the lowest-ranking members surrounding it. Bastian didn't want to listen to his prisoners scream all night long.

As Marcelle marched me along, a few people poked their heads out of their houses, curious to see the alpha's traitorous daughter. There was a mix of reactions. Those loyal to my father sneered and spat. Others looked fearful. And a few looked sad—one or two even angry.

Something pricked my awareness: the realization that none of the women wore shoes. My stomach cramped. I didn't have shoes on either. I never did on pack territory because my father thought it would keep me from running. But now, *none* of the women were allowed?

Marcelle's lip curled as he followed my line of sight. "*You* cost them that privilege. You, and you alone. They all despise you."

My shoulders curled in as if wings could spring from my back and protect me from the onslaught of the words. It did no good. The knowledge that the women of this pack were being hurt because of me sliced me to my bones.

"Keep it moving," Marcelle said, shoving me forward by my head.

I stumbled, my feet sticking in the mud, but I kept moving. I took in the cabins through the mossy trees. They got nicer and larger the closer we got to the main house—Bastian's home. It loomed in the distance.

It stuck out like a sore thumb against the more rustic cabins: white paint and columns that gleamed amid the swampy backdrop. It didn't fit. Just like my father didn't—fake and not true to its nature.

But Marcelle didn't guide me toward it. Instead, he turned me. That's when I saw them—torches lighting the darkening sky and forming a circle.

That twisting sensation was back in my stomach for a whole new reason now.

Two massive bonfires roared on either side of the circle, with a dais of sorts behind it. A chair like a throne loomed highest, snarling wolves carved into the posts and battle scenes playing out on the legs as my father sat impassively atop it, a woman kneeling at his feet.

I lifted my chin, refusing to be cowed by his flair for the dramatic. I would meet whatever he had planned head-on. I would not cower.

Marcelle shoved me toward the dais. I stumbled, but I didn't fall.

Bastian's gaze skimmed over me. "Little Flower, you're looking a little worse for wear."

I didn't make a sound; just stared at him.

His lips twitched. "Such defiance in you. Such fire. It's surprising, really. Maybe there is hope for the line that comes from you yet. But you'll have to prove yourself."

Marcelle scoffed, but I pretended I couldn't hear.

Bastian's fingers drummed on the arm of his chair, his many rings glittering in the firelight. "If you succeed, you'll receive a shower, a meal, and a bed for the night. If you fail, it's back to the pit for another week."

I didn't let hope show on my face. It would bring Bastian too much pleasure.

"But you'll have to win it," he growled.

Dread pooled low in my stomach. *Win it.*

I knew what that meant. The torches. The bonfires. The gathering pack.

They lived for these nights—the bloody battles that entertained Bastian and could earn them favor for a fleeting moment.

But I was a submissive, and the past three days of torment had left me weak, my strength fleeting.

Bastian reached out a hand to grab the kneeling woman's chin and lifted it. "Tell me, pet. Will you fight for my honor?"

"Yes, Alpha," she whispered demurely. But I saw her muscles ripple as she spoke. Everything about her was a finely honed machine.

"Rise, Lilli," Bastian commanded.

She did so gracefully, and my mouth went dry. The woman had at least a foot on me, and as she stretched, I saw that I'd been right about that muscle. The scars across her knuckles told me she was no stranger to a fight.

Bastian leveled his stare at me. "You will fight for the privilege of my shelter. You will fight until death itself comes knocking."

CHAPTER TWO

Kingston

I stared into the fire as it crackled. It should've been too warm to have one, but the Colorado mountains had turned bitterly cold surprisingly early this year—as if the mountains, too, were grieving the loss of Wren, crying out for her return. My wolf howled inside me, raging against the walls I'd constructed around him.

There was no way I could set him free right now. I didn't trust him not to turn feral and run straight for Louisiana. He'd head right to Wren and get us all killed in the process.

The pacing footsteps behind me grated, with their panicked quickness and desperate back-and-forth. I didn't think Puck had stopped moving since Wren disappeared. "We need to move," he growled.

I didn't turn; I just kept staring into the fire as if it held all the answers in the world. "We need a plan. We need to know for sure if Wren is on pack territory, and we need reinforcements."

To anyone else, my voice would sound as if it held no emotion at all. Only I knew that each word was filled with agony. Failure. Guilt. Emotional destruction of the highest order.

The clicking sound intensified, spurred on by my words. "I'm trying," Locke growled. "Their system is good, but if I can hack into their security cameras, I'll at least know what we're walking into."

After the fire, we'd tracked the Red River wolves to the airstrip north of town. But that's where their scents—and Wren's—had disappeared. Locke had done his thing and hacked into the flight records. They'd tried to cover their tracks by flying to Texas and then Kentucky, but the private plane's final destination had been a small town several hours outside New Orleans. I knew in my bones that Bastian had taken her back to Red River.

A fresh wave of agony slammed into me. Wren, at the hands of a monster, the same man who had done such damage to my sister that she'd taken her life. My mind couldn't help but invent the worst images of Wren enduring all that and more.

My fingers tightened around the edge of the stone fireplace mantel. A crack sounded, and the rock beneath my hand crumbled to dust.

A palm landed on my shoulder, fingers squeezing. I knew by scent that it was the one person I least expected, Brix, the man Wren had healed in untold ways. Someone who'd been so averse to any touch that wasn't painful now sought to comfort me.

"It's not your fault," he whispered.

I shoved out of his hold and stalked away. Puck may have had it right with all the pacing. "Ender, anything from your source?"

He shook his head, his expression completely impassive. "He's pulling all his usual lines. I'll hear back as soon as he has something."

Fuck.

Every second we did nothing was another that Wren lived in agony. My vision went blurry as fury surged. I moved without thinking, letting out a roar as I grabbed the antique coffee table and hurled it at the wall.

It splintered into countless pieces, shattering glasses of drinks and plates of uneaten food with it. The whole room went silent. The only sounds were the pieces of my destruction settling and the fire's crackles and pops.

My chest heaved as I dragged in ragged breaths. It wasn't enough. Nothing was. I'd failed Wren in the worst possible way, and now she was paying the price.

I charged toward the hutch against the wall, needing to shatter that, too. Puck, Brix, and Ender all moved in, Brix and Ender grabbing my arms as I battled against them, snarling and snapping.

"Fuck," Puck muttered. "Should I get a tranq?"

We kept them in the medical room in case one of us slipped into a feral state, but the idea of him injecting me with one now only had me fighting harder.

Ender cursed. "Yes. Get it. Now!"

"Wait!" Locke yelled. "I'm in."

Those two words ignited the barest amount of hope in me. A lead. Information. Something that could help us get Wren back safely.

The urge to fight slid clean out of me. Brix and Ender kept a hold of me, waiting to see if it was a false submission, but it wasn't. After a few seconds, they released me.

I scrubbed a hand over my face. "I'm sorry. I—"

"Bugger off," Puck muttered. "I hated that table anyway."

I wanted to laugh, but I couldn't make the sound. Instead, I rounded the couch, wanting to see the computer. The others followed. Locke's fingers alternated between typing and using the trackpad. And then they stilled altogether.

"Fucking hell," he swore, then expanded a camera view.

Wren stood before Bastian, who was on a goddamned throne, but that wasn't what had Locke panicking. It was Wren's back. She faced away from the camera, which had to be tucked in a tree, and wore an oversized T-shirt that should've been white, given the color of the sleeves. Instead, it was stained pink, red, and brown, with a mixture of blood and mud.

Wren's scars played in my mind. Evidence of all the torture she'd endured at her father's hand. And now she was back there. My back teeth gnashed so hard I was fairly certain I'd fractured a molar. But I didn't give a damn. I only had eyes for Wren.

"We have to get her out," Puck rasped. "We can't leave her there."

Brix's breaths came quicker, more ragged. "I…am going… to kill…each and every one of them. I am going to bathe in their blood and put their heads on pikes."

"Locke," Ender said, his voice devoid of all emotion. "Map out every camera location and watchpoint." He looked at me. "They're right. We can't wait any longer."

I knew he was right. It didn't matter that we were up against a pack thirty times the size of ours. We'd find a way. "I'll ready the plane."

My phone rang as I pulled it out, but the sound was a notification for the gate. I frowned and tapped the screen. A familiar face poked out of an SUV window and filled my screen. "Hera? What are you doing here?"

Her pale-green eyes were hard as she stared back at me. "I know how to get her back."

On a station platform, with nothing to read,
and a four-hour train journey stretching ahead of him...

That's where the story began for Penguin founder Allen Lane. With only 'shabby reprints of shoddy novels' on offer, he resolved to make better books for readers everywhere.

By the time his train pulled into London, the idea was formed. He would bring the best writing, in stylish and affordable formats, to everyone. His books would be sold in bookstores, stationers and tobacconists, for no more than the price of a ten-pack of cigarettes.

And on every book would be a Penguin, a bird with a certain 'dignified flippancy', and a friendly invitation to anyone who wished to spend their time reading.

In 1935, the first ten Penguin paperbacks were published. Just a year later, three million Penguins had made their way onto our shelves.

Reading was changed forever.

—

A lot has changed since 1935, including Penguin, but in the most important ways we're still the same. We still believe that books and reading are for everyone. And we still believe that whether you're seeking an afternoon's escape, a vigorous debate or a soothing bedtime story, all possibilities open with a book.

Whoever you are, whatever you're looking for,
you can find it with Penguin.